The Takers and Keepers

Ivan Pope

Hookline Books, Bookline & Thinker Ltd.

He has to live in the midst of the incomprehensible, which is also detestable. And it has a fascination, too, that goes to work upon him. The fascination of the abomination — you know. Imagine the growing regrets, the longing to escape, the powerless disgust, the surrender, the hate.

Joseph Conrad, Heart of Darkness

Hookline Books, Bookline & Thinker
www.hooklinebooks.com

Publisher's Note: This is a work of fiction. Names, characters, places, and incidents are a product of the author's imagination. Locales and public names are sometimes used for atmospheric purposes. Any resemblance to actual people, living or dead, or to businesses, companies, events, institutions, or locales is completely coincidental.

Book Layout © 2021 More Visual

The Takers and Keepers by Ivan Pope. -- 1st ed.
Cover Design: More Visual Ltd
ISBN 9781838057916

For those kept in darkness and those who believe they can never escape.

Descent

Allen was barely awake when the video arrived, but he understood immediately.

You love your keepens, the message said.

He felt sweaty and stale and shook slightly with a sickly shiver. He knew he smelled of a night in the pub and the detritus of sex. In the kitchen his girlfriend worked, marking a pile of schoolbooks for the coming Monday morning. A mug of cold, milky tea and an untouched piece of toast sat just out of reach.

The email contained no message, just a link to a video somewhere out on the internet. He paused a moment to calm his shaking hand. When he clicked through it started automatically and he watched with rapt attention, nodding slowly to himself as the film unfolded.

A video camera, held by an unseen hand, descended slowly into the basement of a house. It panned in the gloom and travelled deeper into the space, down staircases and through small rooms. A hand pushed open a doorway hidden behind a shelving unit and entered the space beyond. At a metal grill the hand pushed it open and proceeded into a small opening through the wall. The descent continues down a ladder. A feeble light illuminates the way. The camera peers into the depths as whoever is carrying it proceeds. Eventually the video steadies and looks into the gloom. A space is revealed, the light is better here. It contains kitchen units and a toilet which appears to be plumbed in. At the end of the room is another small opening in the wall. The camera focuses on this opening as a face momentarily appears and then retreats from view. The camera tracks towards the hole and is poked through. Inside, as the images blur to grey in the dark, a light is switched on and three figures squirm at the light, covering their faces with their arms and turning away. There is no soundtrack, but it is clear someone is shouting instructions. The three turn back to the camera and stare at it in terror. One woman, wearing shorts and a bikini top, and two children dressed in pyjamas. They stare, blinking, until suddenly the light is snapped off and the video ends.

'What's that?' asked Emily. She was standing behind him unseen, watching, a schoolbook dangling between her thumb and forefinger. She bent closer, trying to see the screen. He moved quickly to shut the video down but he was too slow and the awkward attempt at concealment revealed his excitement. She had come in to ask if he wanted to go out for a coffee, but this had now been swept from her mind. Normally he wouldn't mind, he rather relished any interest in his stuff, but not this, this was too raw.

'What the fuck was it?' she repeated.

'Someone just sent it to me,' he said. 'I don't know, nothing much.'

Why did he have to pretend anything? She knew instinctively it was very much more. He slowly clicked the laptop shut as she said, 'But what was it? Someone in a cellar?'

He had almost forgotten how to breathe. He couldn't answer for fear of revealing the state he had been tipped into, his lungs empty of air while his mind raced for answers.

'Holy fuck,' she said, louder now. 'You look like you've seen a ghost.'

A ghost. Exactly. That was it. He had seen a ghost. He knew he had turned white, as white as the human in the film. He felt sweaty and shivery and would lie down to recover if she wasn't standing behind him, waiting for an explanation. All the blood had drained from his head and a wave of nausea swept over him.

'It's nothing. Nothing important. Something for work, maybe. Someone trying to frighten me. Or make me laugh.'

His attempt to shake her off didn't work but she wouldn't fight over it, not in the glow of a Sunday morning.

'I hate that stuff,' she said. 'Your mysterious work.'

2

'It's not funny, I know that,' he agreed.

Go away, go away, go away he thought.

'You know what I mean. All that crap, missing kids, abductors and probably Osama bin Laden hiding in a cave somewhere. It scares me and I really hate it.'

He turned and stared at her. Did he really know her, was he in love with her, how does this thing work, he wondered? He couldn't really be bothered to fight. It can't take much of an effort to understand what I'm doing, he thought.

'I know,' he said, 'I'm sorry.' Not wanting to concede any ground, he could only repeat the same bland apology.

She stood there a few moments longer, waiting for him to soften and reach out, but he was lost to her now, willing her departure so he could take another look. It's been a long time coming, he thought, I can wait a few more minutes. Finally, she walked out of the room in silence, leaving an unpleasant absence. He felt relieved but at the same time he hated himself for forcing her away. Quickly he flipped his machine open again, but when it reconnected, he was surprised by the message.

This video has been removed by its owner.

Allen

Sundays were a day of slow-motion progress, from bed to bar to lunch and back to bed again with Emily. She was a pleasure. He knew he was onto a long-term thing, finally.

He usually tried not to let himself get distracted by emails before he was showered and dressed in the morning, but some days it was easy to give in to the vicarious pleasure of the screen. He hadn't really been reading any emails, just skimming the spam and the junk that waited for his attention and hitting the delete key. He had work to do, a short piece to finish for *The Times*, and something longer to get started on for the Americans, *The Journal of Familial Depravity*. That would be harder, he thought. They would want proper references, the sort of deep research that he didn't normally have the time or inclination for. He opened up the partly written document, but his attention quickly drifted back to the video.

After a long period of drift, Allen had ended up in North London, determined to sort out a way forward. Islington was a place he'd never been to before jail, but he liked it for its easy lifestyle and the anonymity of its residents. People came and went with rapidity, that was good. He didn't have to get to know anyone, they left him alone. Then he met and paired up with a sweet girl, Emily Morgan. She was a teacher, small children. She knew from the first about his past and his time inside, he told her on their first night together, anticipating, perhaps, a longer relationship, or maybe relishing a chance to admit his past. He didn't want anything hanging over his head.

Anyway, Islington suited them both with its coffee shops, boutiques, pubs. Although he hadn't known it before, it turned out to be his sort of life; the drift along busy streets, meetings in cafes, nights in the pub. He even became gregarious, friended, under her spell. He knew people again and he liked them, looked forward generally to seeing them. Her teaching job was in a local school, easy to get to from where they lived.

Neither of them was originally a Londoner, but in the way of generations of incomers they'd become attached to the life and the opportunities it offered.

They rented a basement flat with a tiny garden and a gravelled space at the front where an old taxicab was parked. He had somehow acquired the cab along with the flat. The previous tenant, not wanting to take it to his new property, had proposed leaving it with him in return for an outstanding electricity bill. He'd been trying to work out what to do with it ever since.

It suited him fine, this life, this flat in an old house. They had one large bedroom and one small second bedroom, box room really, that he used as a study. A kitchenette at the back opened out onto a garden which was more of a walled yard than a proper garden. He hadn't ever been the gardening type, but he'd taken to this scrap of land and created a space full of interesting plants in assorted pots. He couldn't name any of them, but he was amazed at his own creativity, something he'd previously put down as vaguely sissy in others. In the summer he spent long hours sitting out here, writing or marking up printouts of articles.

He liked it here, he liked this life. He liked the slow, relentless gathering of information, getting it into some sort of order and then forcing a story from the fragments. He never would have thought he could be a writer, but he seemed to have become one almost by mistake. In the army, keeping notebooks would have been insane and led to bullying. Even when he started writing properly, making attempts at writing about his life, he'd never thought it could be serious. After leaving the army he'd worked as a labourer and run a few scams with mates, serious stuff but nothing worth writing home about. He assumed, like his brothers, that he'd fall into some job where his body did the work and his brain was saved for the pub or the bookies. It was unexpected, the slow drift to brain work, but when it came it was unstoppable. He soon had a subject and an audience and didn't look back.

It was the same with Emily. She wasn't really his type, or maybe she was. From an academic family who had pushed her to go through university, she'd come out the other end as a schoolteacher. Not, he thought, that there was anything wrong with being a schoolteacher, but he knew that if he'd had a chance to go to college he wouldn't have ended up as a teacher.

He ran a hot bath into which he tipped half a bottle of bubbles. Feeling a bit detached from the world, he lay in the foam thinking about the video. He wished he'd paid it more attention, that he hadn't been distracted. He was almost buried in foam when Emily came into the bathroom and gestured to him.

'I'm sorry I snapped at you.'

That was par for the course. She bent down to take a kiss, a peck on the lips, a settlement of their spat. He didn't reply, not wanting to be hijacked into forgiveness, still angry that she couldn't see what he saw. He tried to dismiss her with silence, scared to draw her anywhere near his thoughts. She stood her ground and looked at him as he steeped in the bubbles.

'I know it's your work, I'm sorry. I'm not judging you, but it scares me. I'm not going to pretend. I just don't like it.'

He sighed and turned his eyes up to meet hers. She always ambushed him when he was vulnerable, when he couldn't escape. He stared at her body, realising he now wanted to fuck her. He closed his eyes to escape her gaze.

'Listen, let's talk later. I'm tired. You know what, I need this story, but if it freaks you out, I'll leave it. Your choice, you tell me.'

He tailed off, not wanting to push home his advantage. There was a fundamental difference between them, they knew that. He felt like he'd done too much, seen too much, while she sometimes seemed like a child, fresh out of school. She looked for a quiet life with time to concentrate on her career, hang out with her friends, walk in the hills. She had what he considered strange hobbies: orienteering, rock-climbing. He'd never been one for separate interests and he didn't really understand what these things, that she'd brought with her from a previous existence, meant. He felt tolerated in that scheme of things but he knew he was not ready to give her up. He didn't mind annoying her to get his way, but he didn't want to push her away. There was a calmness in this relationship, the first time he'd known that sort of peace.

'You'll never give it up,' she said. 'Not even if I ask you to. I don't know why you find it so titillating.'

Not titillating he thought, that's the wrong word. He looked at her through half-closed eyes.

'I thought you weren't going to be like that today.'

She scowled and turned to leave the room.

'There is something at the end of it all,' he said.

'Only you,' she said, 'that's what's at the end of it. Allen fucking Kimbo, always one more lead, one more person to save. You fuck me up, Allen. What you need is a proper job.'

And that was the sentence he hated most.

'You don't have to do this. Nobody asked you to do penance for them.'

Silence.

'You've done your time. Get out of the shadows.'

He laughed. 'It's not personal. It's my job, following this stuff. There are real victims, out there. Nobody else gives a fuck for them, do they? That's what I'm doing.'

Her face creased, but she held her lips together as she had learned as a girl.

'I love you, baby. You do what you have to do and I'll wait for you to get finished.'

She bent, kissed him lightly on the forehead and was gone.

Please don't get involved, she had said.

He'd started his writing career with crap speculative pieces for the trash press and moved on to authoritative pieces for the quality press, when they'd have them. But he had his subject almost to himself, nobody else wanted to cover his beat: the missing and the lost, abductees and prisoners, who disappeared from the world and seldom resurfaced. He'd slowly built up a network of contacts, from prison officers to bent policemen, social workers and probation officers, gangsters and paedophiles. At the start he really had no idea how to find contacts or what they wanted from him, but after a few false starts he'd come to realise that every contact needed something in return. As the work increased and he found he had some spare cash, he fell into a routine of discovering the reward that each source of information wanted. Of course, it wasn't always cash. In fact, money seldom changed hands. The cons wanted phone cards or, more recently, actual phones smuggled in. The coppers wanted trips to strip clubs or drinking sessions in dark boozers. The social workers wanted nothing at all, apart from maybe covering the cost of petrol and an affirmation of their importance. Whatever, he was happy to play the mind games that built layer on layer his web of contacts. He had a lot of contacts, for sure, and he had inside knowledge of events. But they seldom led to anything concrete.

At first his subject was trafficking. Girls, women, men, children. From Moldova and beyond, through Serbia and out across Europe, Ethiopia, Nigeria and beyond. Girls, women, boys, men. Mothers, fathers, children. Brothers and sisters. People traded as if they were drugs, alongside drugs, with drugs inside them, for drugs.

Drugs can be consumed once, but a woman can be consumed hundreds of times. Traded women were much more valuable than pharmaceuticals, and the authorities were seldom interested. A shivering wreck of a human with fear knocked into her over months or years is hardly likely to tell a passing policeman that she never chose this life, that she was abducted at fifteen from her parents' farm and taken from city to city, fucked by a thousand paying customers.

He was a self-made expert on the global phenomenon of human bondage, and a specialist on the trafficking from Eastern to Western Europe. It was a trade more valuable than the heroin business, in which the rewards were huge and the punishments tiny when caught. Although the authorities had been working to break the networks for years, they were ineffectual and corrupted in many arenas.

And beyond the usual trafficking of human flesh, there were deeper and darker processes.

For years he'd followed rumours of the existence of photographs of incarcerated adults and children, entire families that were created underground. He knew there were some very sick people around – they existed in prisons around Europe and the Americas. Each big story that broke in the international press reinforced his belief that something deeper was going on. The Fritzl case, Priklopil, paedophile rings and sex attack kidnappings. Each brought him more clues, but he could never open the door to the network.

He had many scraps of information but no whole picture.

He had been collecting stories of abducted and disappeared people for over five years. As well as a thick file, he had thousands of internet links, fragments of conversations, possible clues and hints of connections.

He believed that there were many more people held long term than the authorities admitted. He knew it was happening and he had some idea of the worst offenders, a group who helped each other take and keep victims..

They called these captives *keepen.*

He settled at his desk in the small back room he used as an office. Sun streamed in, highlighting dust that glowed in response. Spring was turning to summer, but the days were still cold. It was a good time of year; things were moving along nicely on the work front. He looked forward to a few months of solid activity, a few trips, visits to crime scenes, a lot of writing and, maybe, progress with a book proposal. He felt it was time to write something more substantive than articles and news stories. He almost had enough material for a real book. He had been thinking about it for a long while, but he was aware he needed something more, something new and unique.

He'd put out feelers, hoping to penetrate deeper into that world. Perhaps this was a result.

The kettle boiling snapped him back from his dreaming. He added ground coffee to the coffee press and poured the boiling water over it. After waiting a few moments, he pushed the plunger down and poured coffee onto the milk. He added a generous spoonful of sugar, stirred and sipped. Hot. He felt it enter his bloodstream while he looked at the email listing, scanning the senders and subjects quickly, looking for the interesting stuff amid the junk. Nothing much, just the continuation of a few conversations and a lot of things that might have been interesting in the past but which now bored him. A lot of things bored him.

Through his distraction he noticed an email from a friend, Peter Jenkins, a funny but somewhat pompous man who edited and owned a popular London magazine, *London Strife*. Peter loved scandal, crime, suffering, drama and celebrities who had strayed.

The email got straight to the point.

Hi Allen, I've got something interesting for you, might be big. Can we talk. Lunch? Peter

Jenkins had a reputation as a chancer, a publisher with a big mouth and an eye for the bigger story that had served him well. Allen trusted him, knew it was no bullshit. He wasn't afraid to print anything, he took risks. For that Allen loved him. He loved the magazine and he loved Jenkins.

Their relationship was complicated. They'd met five or six years previously, soon after Allen came out of prison. Allen was trying to place a couple of pieces he'd written, and Jenkins, recognising something intriguing in him and a raw talent, had taken him under his wing, giving him a series of assignments. As Allen became a better writer, Jenkins took to treating Allen to lunch lunching him and passing on titbits of gossip and intelligence that he'd picked up from his police contacts or links to the ever-changing criminal scene. Allen, on the other hand, was more interested in a seedy demi-monde that was completely alien to Jenkins and constantly tried to drag him towards it. In this way, over time, they formed a powerful alliance. Jenkins provided a home for research that sometimes took months or years to pull together and he opened doors for Allen as he needed them.

He wrote a swift reply.

Your place? tomorrow lunch, see you there. Allen

The offices of *London Strife* were in Fitzrovia, that slice of historic London that sat between Oxford Street and Tottenham Court Road. It didn't take Allen long to get over there. He found Jenkins sitting in the spring sunshine outside a trendy restaurant, Rack, on Charlotte Street. He was wearing a suit, no tie and big sunglasses. Not one to abstain at lunchtime, he was sipping a vodka tonic.

'Allen,' Jenkins said enthusiastically, patting the seat next to him. Allen sat down and they surveyed the street together.

'Drink?' he asked as a waiter emerged.

'No thanks,' Allen said. He didn't really drink these days, that had been part of the problem that had led him into temptation. They both ordered steak frites, rare, before the waiter could get away again.

'So, how's your underworld?' said Jenkins.

'Gloomy,' said Allen. 'Nothing dramatic, just the usual procession of lost daughters and missing sons.'

'Why is it that daughters are lost but sons go missing? And children, what do they do?' said Jenkins.

'Children are always snatched by strangers,' Allen said. 'Even when they're not. Come on, then. What's your big mystery?'

Jenkins laughed and paused for effect.

'I've only got Jennifer fucking Ransome.'

Jennifer Ransome. Allen knew the story well. Twelve years after disappearing she had walked back out of history, large as life, all grown up. Came into a police station in Holloway two months before and told them who she was and that she wanted to go home. They had no fucking idea. She'd been gone for so long, there was a whole new generation of police. The guy who had led the search was long retired. The press went crazy as she was swept up into a safe house and closeted with police liaison and psychiatrists, doctors, family, the works. But no press. No stories had leaked, no photos either. She was a blank, a fascinating, tantalising, blank.

Jenkins sipped his vodka. 'You know it was always my story?'

Allen nodded. 'Of course, but how …'

'I know her parents well. I talked to them a lot after she went missing. At first, I was just another reporter, but, after a few months, when everybody thought she was dead, I kept on plugging away, asking questions, demanding her return. I did think she was dead, I always thought that, but I couldn't admit it to her mum and dad. I'd got too close. I kept telling them, she might have run away, with a boy or something. It wasn't very likely, she was too young, but we grasped at straws. It didn't seem to do any harm. The weeks passed, then the months, and eventually I think we all decided that she was dead, but we never said it out loud. It sort of became the great unfinished business of *London Strife*, of my life really. I carried some guilt, tell you the truth, that I'd gone on so long about her being alive, but in the end the story drifted away. You can't keep focussed on one person like that, and the mag had started to grow, we had a lot of other stories, we were learning our trade. In the end, though I never lost touch with them completely, I moved on. I'm not sure they ever moved on, even by one day.' Allen looked at Jenkins' expensive suit. He sure had moved on, he thought, on the backs of these stories.

'And now?' he said, not wanting to spend the whole of lunch rehashing old stories.

'Now? Now it turns out they never forgot me, and when she reappeared, they called me first. Anyway, eat up. How's the steak?'

'Steak's good. Tell me about this girl.'

'She's not a girl anymore. She's grown up. I'm not sure what happened to her, you'd think she would be broken, but …'

'But?'

'It's hard to explain. She's motoring. She's got ambition, like she wants to be fucking famous. Get on the telly.'

'Well, good for her,' said Allen.

He paused.

'But what's that got to do with me?'

'Well, she needs someone to write her book, of course. You know, ghost her story. I thought you could do it.'

A ghost for a ghost, he thought, and his pulse quickened. Of course. This was the book, he thought, that he'd been waiting for.

He knew Jennifer's story was valuable. Everybody wanted to know what horrors had gone on, where she'd been held, what indignities she had been subjected to: the usual prurient interest masquerading as public interest. The media had speculated with abandon, but barely any word leaked from the Ransome camp. The police filled in a few of the gaps for their favoured contacts and promised a press conference, maybe even Jennifer herself, 'in good time'. Denied their story, the press made up whatever they wanted, harassed any relatives or friends of the family they could find and constructed elaborate graphics on the basis of their guesswork. Forensic artists were brought in to make impressions of what she might look like now, impressions that varied so much from paper to paper as to be a joke. Nobody really knew what had happened, nobody really knew what was happening.

Allen gripped Jenkins' arm hard, convinced for a moment he was joking. 'Why would she want me?'

'Her mum wants her to be happy. And there's money in it, lots of money. We've got an agent, we'll set up an auction for the rights. It's just a fixed-fee job – and your name on the cover. Below hers, of course.'

'So, is it true?'

'True?'

'That stuff, any of it? The stories?'

It was said that she was quite mad, that she had three dwarf children, that she talked in a strange language, that she had twenty-inch fingernails and white hair. It was also said that she was preparing a media career, that she had signed up as a columnist with a red top and that she would be a contestant on *Celebrity Big Brother*.

'That's what you'll find out, I guess. All I've heard is that she was talking to the police and the doctors and that she got the hump for some reason and moved out of hospital and is holed up with her parents in a rented house somewhere. The papers are sniffing around, my guess is that they will find her soon, so you better get a move on. Her parents have given me first sniff, for old times' sake.'

He giggled. 'Does that sound sick?'

'She's not stupid, you know. The press is going crazy for her and everyone wants to know what happened. To see her. If she wants to write a book, and she wants you to help her write the book, then you fucking get in there and write the book.'

The waiter returned. Jenkins went quiet. When he had gone, Jenkins continued.

'There's another thing. A copper, Herman. He's a Detective Constable now, thinks he owns the case.'

'And?'

'Well, we've been sparring over this for a long time. When she went, he was just a spotty plod in a hat, but now he's serious, a real detective. He's already warned me off the case.' Jenkins smiled. 'Do you understand?'

He was serious now. 'Herman can fuck this story up for us unless we're smart. But you're a professional, it's your job. And it's your big break. You keep everyone happy and I'll sort us out a contract.'

'Since when were you my manager?' said Allen quietly, under his breath. But he knew that, if the book was going to be written, he would make sure he was the one who wrote it.

Jennifer

Two days later, Allen took a bus out through East London to the leafy edge of the city. Through nervousness he got off the bus too early and, holding a scrap of paper with an address on it, walked for a while, getting more depressed as he went. Family cars sped past, sending dust into the air while the occasional mother pushing a buggy passed him by.

Eventually he found the long, quiet road lined with houses that looked very run-down, standing behind spindly hedges stunted by the grimy traffic fumes. When he got to the house, he double-checked the number on a gatepost and walked up the path past an overgrown front garden. He rang the doorbell and listened as it jangled in the distance. After a short delay the door was opened by a middle-aged woman wearing leather trousers and a top with *Vogue* marked out in pink sparkles. She wore a lot of makeup and was holding a small dog by the collar, which put her into an uncomfortable, half-stooped stance.

He smiled broadly at her. 'Mrs Ransome?'

'Yes,' she said blankly and smiled back.

He held out his hand. 'Allen Kimbo. I've come to talk to Jennifer. I'm the writer, it's about her book? I phoned.'

She seemed to finally get it and, ignoring his hand, nodded him in across the hallway towards the front room. It was large and overheated, violently carpeted and filled with furniture, people and a smoky fug. Allen edged in sideways while the woman who'd answered the door pushed in behind him.

'Don't worry about them, Mr Allen, things are a bit hectic but they're just family. Mostly.'

She spoke into the room, loudly. 'Everyone, this is Allen. He's come to talk to Jenni. She might be writing a book.'

Everybody in the room looked at him with a certain expectation. He half-expected them to give a round of applause, but they just clucked in approval, as if he was a publisher come to announce a gifted daughter's first novel.

He said that he understood what they'd been through, though of course he didn't.

'I'm sorry about the crowd,' said Mrs Ransome. 'This is my sister. Her husband. My oldest. It's his birthday.'

'And this is Mr Soanes, our new lawyer.'

Mr Soanes grinned broadly and waved a wine glass at him in a friendly gesture.

She waved vaguely at the rest of the people present who smiled back at him in turn and returned to their conversations.

'Let's go to the kitchen,' she said. 'I expect you'd like a cup of tea.'

The kitchen was empty. He sat at a small table by a window while she busied herself with the kettle. He looked out at a large back garden and a small tiled area littered with dog faeces.

'Nice house,' he said.

'Yes, isn't it just? The government are paying for it, for therapy they said, for the best. For now, anyway. They said we needed to be away from everyone. Jenni likes it, she likes the garden.'

'You must be very glad to have her back,' he said.

'I still can't believe it, but I don't think I'll ever get over it. All those years, gone, empty.' She looked away. 'You know, although you always have to say you believe she's still alive, I didn't really. Not at all. I just gave up hope, years ago, otherwise I would have gone mad. My doctor told me: "Julie," he said, "Julie, you've got to face up to facts." When I asked him what he meant he said: "She's gone, you know, and she isn't coming back." He was wrong, wasn't he? But I believed him after that. I didn't say it to anyone, but I did. I thought she'd gone for good, into the ground.'

She took a mug from the cupboard.

'She's like a different girl now, all grown up and knowing what she wants to do. I don't really know her – don't tell her I said that – but sometimes it's like a miracle from god. It's come as a shock, I'll say. Her brother, well, he didn't really know her, he was only tiny when she went, but he's happy. I say happy, he's a bit confused. But he'll get used to it. Even the vicar has been round, you know. He said I need to get back to church. Funny, isn't it? I stopped going, years ago, and he never visited all those years, but I don't think I could start again now. Do you think I should go back? Is there any point? I've got her back and all.'

Her voice had become high-pitched, volatile. She stopped to take a breath. He could feel the stress coming off her.

'I see what you mean,' he said. 'Maybe it's just a reaction to her, um, time away. All those years on her own, it doesn't bear thinking about.'

He hesitated, not sure where this was going. 'I imagine she spent a lot of time thinking about you.'

Mrs Ransome twisted her handkerchief in her lap. 'It's the doctors, they wanted us, her, to be safe. But you know ...' And she looked behind her to check in case anyone had entered the kitchen, '... you know, the newspaper wanted to send us to a hotel. In London. They said they would pay for everything, and Jenni could do some interviews. But the doctors, they didn't want us to do that. I would have liked a hotel, although this house is very nice. But it scares me, at night, it's too quiet.'

'What did Jenni want to do?'

'Well, she's got her own plans, that one. It's as if she came back with plans. But she won't tell me, she won't listen to me on anything now. I suppose she's an adult, but it seems strange to me. I never got to see her grow up, never got to teach her anything, and now I'm going to lose her all over again.'

He felt pity for this woman, dragged along her whole life by forces she was not in control of.

'My husband won't talk about it, but then he won't talk to anyone, poor love, he's not been well. It's this television thing that I'm worried about, it seems all wrong to me, that she could go on television and, well, I'm not sure if even she knows what. Become some sort of television person and have her own programme and everything. Where did that come from, that's what I want to know?'

He wasn't sure whether he was taking advantage or if this was what she wanted. Play it by ear, he thought, go where it leads. She opened the kitchen door and they stepped out onto the tiny concrete patio. She pointed to some lichen covered plastic garden chairs and they both sat down again. Mrs Ransome lit a cigarette. Allen pulled out a digital recorder.

She reached over and pressed down with her fingertips on his wrist.

'You know, I didn't think she would ever come back. I really didn't. I waited such a long time. I didn't want to give in, but inside I did. Every year we still did our ceremony, on the anniversary, and on her birthday, but in the end, you just give up believing – can you understand that?'

'Of course,' he said.

'She was my little one and I lost her and then I tried to forget about her. And then she came back. Can you, can you ...' She looked around nervously, as if somebody might be listening, then drew deeply on her cigarette.

'How is it, between you and her?' he said.

'Strange thing was, I had a dream about her the night before she appeared. I hadn't dreamed about her for years. Then I seemed to spend the whole night chasing her in and out of this old building.'

She laughed. 'You know how dreams are, first we were standing on the street, on the high street here, where we used to go shopping together. Then I turned around and she was gone. But I knew it was a dream. Even so, I panicked, I thought, what if I wake up and I could have found her and I haven't. I set off where I thought she'd gone, into the shopping centre, but every time I got near her, I lost sight of her again. Funny isn't it, how dreams do that to you? I woke up with a very strange feeling that morning, like I now knew what had happened to her, that she was alright. The truth of it was, year on year, I never stopped wondering where she was but I never thought the worst. And then she came back to me, just like that.'

Allen made sympathetic noises.

She pulled another cigarette from the packet and lit it quickly. 'I really should give these things up. What with the dream and everything, and it was a bad time and I was feeling a down. I just cried, at first, when she came back. I didn't want to believe it. But then, when I was sure, then I started thinking even worse things. I was scared, I don't mind admitting. She was fifteen when she went, and now she'd be in her twenties, and I'd never clapped eyes on her all that time. I didn't know who she was, or what was she coming home to. Or who was coming home. What I'd dreamed of and wanted for so long, suddenly came true, and it made me feel stupid. Stupid.'

She looked into the distance with a thousand-yard stare.

'She won't really talk to me now, though.' She seemed close to tears. 'She pretends everything is alright, when other people are around. But she doesn't really want to talk to me. I lost my girl, my baby, what I got back, I don't know.'

'I'm sorry.'

'Well, you don't have to be sorry, Mr Allen,' she said, and burst into tears. Then she stopped as suddenly as she had started, pulled out a tissue and blew her nose. 'I hope you won't put that in your book,' she said.

Allen realised this was taking them around in circles.

'Can I talk to Jennifer then?'

'Of course you can, my love, but please keep it short. And be nice to her. She's got some crazy ideas, but we do love her, we don't want her hurt. Not anymore.'

He followed her up the narrow stairs to a landing. They passed a bathroom smelling of damp flannels and mildew. At the top of the stairs Mrs Ransome went up to a closed door and pushed it slowly open, warily. 'Hello Jen,' she said. 'I've got that nice writer man here to talk to you.' She reached back and tugged at Allen's elbow. 'You go on in,' she whispered.

He stepped part way into the room. The curtains were shut but several dim lights were on. His eyes took time to adjust. The room was stuffed with belongings, bags piled around a bed, shelves laden with books, trinkets and boxes. A three-bar heater was on, space carved out for it at the end of the bed, with more bags piled precariously around and dangerously close to the hot elements. Jennifer's mother hovered behind him.

A young woman sat on the far end of the bed in the gloom.

'Hello Jennifer,' he said cautiously. No reply. 'Jenni. Hey.' He took two cautious steps into the room, still holding on to the door handle as he did so, trying to find spaces for his feet in the clutter and feeling he was in danger of toppling into the mess.

He could see her, but she still didn't respond as he clambered further into the room. He grinned inanely, suddenly feeling stupid.

'I've come to talk about your book.' He paused. 'If that's what you want. Your mum said you did.'

He didn't know whether to talk to her as a child or an adult. The heat was getting to him, there was a deep, earthy, pungent smell in the room which almost made him gag. Still she didn't respond. He froze, willing a response from the figure in front of him.

Then, from the doorway, her mother piped up.

'Jen dear, this is the man I told you about. From the magazine, Mr Jenkins' friend. You asked me to bring him, didn't you? Don't be silly now, dear.'

Suddenly she made a strange sound. 'Ch, ch, chey. You can sit where you want,' she said.

Her voice was calm and strong, a bit childish with a strange lisp crossed with a stammer. He'd spent a lot of time wondering what she'd look like, but he hadn't anticipated how she'd sound. He took another step into the room, tempted now to jump from hummock to hummock. She turned around and looked straight at him and smiled.

'Hello Jennifer,' he said, more boldly now.

She was a large girl, not fat but big-boned with flesh over the bones. She was wearing a skirt and striped top and makeup, as if she'd taken time over her appearance. Not the small waifish child he'd been imagining; she was an adult wearing modern clothes.

He tried not to stare as he took in her elegant hair, styled and coloured with a silver and brown peppering, something rather trendy about it all, or maybe old-fashioned, he thought. He re-alised he didn't know much about hair styles. She was clutching a tiny blue mobile phone. On the bed next to her was a laptop. He looked around for somewhere to sit and she patted the side of the bed next to herself. He climbed quickly over the bags and sat himself on the corner of the bed. He smiled at her, a large, friendly smile, intended to calm her down. Her mother hung around at the door, silent but watchful, a chaperone for her returned daughter. He was starting to sweat in the close heat of this room, he could feel the pricks of it on his scalp.

'Mummy, you can leave us, thank you.'

It was the voice of an adult but with a lilt to it, as if it had been learned from watching American television.

He stared at the young woman sitting on the bed. She had a large, long face, somewhat like her mother's. Her face was drawn and pale and she looked young despite the makeup.

She stared at him. 'What's the matter? Do you think I should look like a troll?'

For a moment he didn't know how to respond. He was get-ting dozy in the close heat of the room. Then he laughed. 'Actually, you look great,' he said.

This broke the tension and she smiled in return. 'I don't know what your name is.'

'It's Allen,' he said.

'OK, Allen, what are we going to do?'

'We're going to write a book?' he said. 'To write your book. Is that what you want?'

She stared at him. 'Will you be nice to me? If you're going to write my book and I'm going to tell the world, then you'll have to be nice to me. I'm not going to hide anymore.'

'You don't have to hide,' he said, thinking that she did, probably.

'I know I don't have to,' she shot back. 'This is part of our plan; I dreamed this a lot, for a long time. I knew you would come after he let me out, don't think you are so clever. When I stopped dreaming, when it got real, I didn't like it. It's been a long time, is all.'

Allen wasn't sure where to start.

'Would you like to talk about it?'

'I want to get on television.'

'I understand that,' he said, 'but first we must write your book. You have to help me; you have to tell me stuff. We'll do it together.'

She sat in silence for a few minutes. 'Aylen, promise you will listen to me and only write what I say.'

'I will do my best,' he said. He felt completely adrift in the face of someone who'd been held captive for twelve years.

'It's my birthday soon.'

'How old will you be?' he said.

'I forgot.'

That was the child.

'Can you remember how it started?' he tried. 'We could start with that. Or how you got out, if you like.'

A long silence. He was beginning to wonder if she'd fallen asleep on him.

'Can you get me on the telly?' she said.

'Probably anything if you want, but you'll have to give me some help because I can't do anything for you if you won't talk to me.'

'Do you write for *The Sun*? What sort of a writer are you, anyway? Writing about dead people? Writing about fucked-up people, is that what you do?'

'I'm just a writer. I try to write about people who have problems, who have been lost – like you, I guess. I don't write for *The Sun*. Do you think I should?'

She thought about this for a long time and Allen wondered what was going through her mind. He had talked to other returnees and knew the sort of things they struggled with. He understood the darkness of it, he didn't shy away from that, the second-hand struggle to emerge from the dark chambers. But he also enjoyed letting light into spaces where no light had shone. He never knew where it would lead.

'OK.' Her voice had changed now, become more girlish. 'Come on then.'

'Come on what?'

'I will tell you the bad things. I'm not scared anymore.'

He started to feel she was playing games with him.

He hadn't intended to do much more than have a chat with her, but he could feel the tension in the air. Allen slowly pulled his recorder from a pocket and placed it on the bed.

'Want to start now?'

She grinned at him. 'I've got a lot to say. I've been practising. What do you want me to tell?'

'Well, how about you tell me how it all started – what you can remember.'

She made a little noise like a strangled laugh. 'He got me when I was on my way to school. A horrid man, but that's not what I thought when I met him. I liked him, he was funny at first. He took me to live with him in his flat, but when we got there he wouldn't let me go, he made me live in a garage. Or a cellar, I'm not sure. A room, anyway. And he didn't have any children or pets, or even a wife. He just lived on his own. And he was mean.'

She sniffled violently, as if she was about to burst into tears. He waited for her to go on.

'He took me up to his house.'

Up.

23

'And he threw me into this little room; he told me I had to stay there. Then he turned off all the lights and left me for a long time. That's how it all started. He left me and I cried and cried for a few days, then he came back with some food and I was so hungry I said thank you.'

'Tell me a bit more about him,' he said.

She folded slowly down onto the bed and lay on her side, placing her hands under her head, staring up at the ceiling as if trying to see things.

'It was a long time ago. I was only little, but even then I knew it was wrong, what he was doing. I wanted to go home to my mum. I wanted that so much, I would lie in the dark and think about my mum and try to make her know I was still alive. You know I lived with him for years. Years and years. You get used to it, you get used to anything really, and he turned out quite funny. He could make me laugh. We watched television together, and he looked after me. He made me my favourite food, but for a long time he never let me out of his house.'

'What about this room, what was it like?'

Her voice was getting quieter, smaller. 'It was dark and cold and smelly. And I had to live in it for a long, long time. More time than I can remember. At first he was not nice to me, and he made the room horrible, but when we became friends he let me make it a bit nicer.'

He wanted to ask what she meant, not nice. He realised this was dangerous ground. If felt as if she was challenging him to question this. He pressed on, keeping his feelings under control.

'He became your friend?'

Jennifer was drifting away, she seemed closed off, locked in a memory of her world. It was hard to work out where to start, but he wanted to get her talking.

'And when you disappeared, what about that? How did it happen?'

'I didn't disappear, you know. I was always there.' She laughed. 'When you say disappeared, it's like you mean I didn't exist anymore, but I did. Did you think I was dead? Mum did, you know. She told everyone I was dead, she lit candles for me. But I wasn't dead. Maybe to Mum and Dad and everyone I wasn't there, but to me I was always there, in my grave, but alive.'

He asked her where they'd walked to and how it had happened and she started to unravel her story, in a jumpy fashion, leaving out detail, ignoring some questions. She rambled a lot, about a day on the buses and buying ice-cream. She had a good memory for something that had happened twelve years before, it seemed.

'He got me on my way to school. Well, I wasn't really on my way to school, I went to the shops and met him in there, sort of, you know. He talked to me in a nice way and we walked down the road talking, you know, sort of friendly. I didn't want to go in to school, I was trying to think of a way to skive off for the day, but I didn't have anywhere to go to. We chatted down the road, you know. I was shy of him.'

'I went with him, I did, really,' she said shyly. 'I quite liked him, after we'd talked a bit and he gave me a packet of cigarettes. I knew I shouldn't really talk to him and go off with him, Mum told me that, but I did because I was in a mood and I was scared of school. He didn't seem scary, he didn't talk down to me like I was a kid, he understood what I was on about and he told me he'd never been to school a lot himself, that he didn't think I should go if I didn't want to. He said I was almost a grown-up and I should start to make my own decisions. After a while I forgot that it was a school day and he was a man that I'd never met before, he didn't seem much older than me and it was like we were friends. Then it was lunchtime and I was hungry and so was he and we laughed a lot and he said would I like to come to his flat for lunch. I didn't really want to, but I didn't know what else to do and by then we were getting on so well that I thought why not? It was like an adventure. We were in a bit of London I didn't really know, that I hadn't been to before, big buildings, not tower blocks, but like that, a poor

25

part of town, poorer than I was used to, but he seemed okay, so we went up to his flat. He made me lunch.'

Allen scratched down a few words and checked his recorder. He didn't want to interrupt the flow.

They watched television, she said. He didn't try anything, but she got nervous.

'I started to feel like he didn't want me to leave. When I said I should be getting home, he talked a lot and he changed the subject so I didn't know what he was saying. He said we could go out for fish and chips later, that he would look after me. I was scared, but I didn't want to show it. I thought I'd got my-self into a stupid situation and I started to worry about what my mum would think when she found out. I said maybe we should go for chips, because I thought that when we were out I could run away from him or shout and ask for help in the shop. Then he said, sure, let's go. He gave me a cup of tea and said I must drink it up before they went, so I gulped it down.'

She stopped talking suddenly. He watched her intently, try-ing to work out what she was thinking. He tried to make out her face, but it was in shadow.

'Alright there?' he said. 'Are you feeling poorly? Do you want to stop for a bit?'

He didn't want to stop, but thought he'd better look after her, take it easy. She seemed in a frail state of mind.

'No, I'm alright,' she said. 'I'm ok, it's just, it's hard to say this, it sounds stupid, but how long was I gone for?'

He felt sorry for her, but couldn't help thinking that he was on the edge of a great story.

'A few years,' he said. 'A lot. People want to find out what you've been doing all that time,' he said.

'Yeah, sure. Do they really?' She seemed to perk up some-what. 'They're interested in me?'

He didn't have the heart to tell her the salubrious nature of this intent. He wondered about his own desire to know, cam-ouflaged and sanctified by his role as journalist.

'What happened to the fish and chips?' he said, restarting the thread.

'We never got fish and chips. I don't know why. I wasn't awake for a long time after that. I don't know what happened. I woke up in a room that I was locked in to, I couldn't open the door. I banged on the door and shouted and nobody ever came. Then I got very scared and I cried, but I felt so sick I couldn't stand up for long. I didn't know that place was my new house.'

'What do you mean, your new house?'

'I had to stay in that room for all the time I was there. I hardly ever got let out again for years and years. Do you think The Prick would let me out, even if I begged him? I stayed in the same place for such a long time. He said it wasn't safe to go out.'

'Why do you call him that?' Allen said.

'The Prick? Because he's a man and he's got a, you know? That's why I call him that. Why do you think? He's the man I met at the shop, the same man.'

'Can you describe him, what did he look like, what did he do every day? Did he have a job?'

She told him she'd been locked in the same room, almost without respite, she said. It was really two rooms, one big and one small. The rooms had no windows. The big room had a bed in it and a bookshelf, though there were no books at first. She said the room was cold sometimes, there was no heating and she would spend all day under a blanket, and sometimes it was very hot and she could hardly breathe. She thought she was at the top of the building they'd gone to on that first day. Other times she came to believe she was in a cellar, though she thought maybe that was only a dream. She could hear noises through the walls sometimes, but she couldn't work out what they were. Her days were spent sleeping and waiting for him to bring her food and water. She was dependent on him for everything. At first, she said, she had nothing, not even a covering for the night, and she slept in her clothes and shivered.

27

She had no clock for the first year and lost track of time. Time had not meant much to her during what she said was her lost time, she'd slept and woken as she needed to.

She'd spent a lot of time at first wondering why nobody was coming to look for her. When she asked The Prick why he would not let her go, he told her that there was a gang of people who stole and killed children, and that he was saving her from that gang.

After a long time, she said, he brought her comics and some books and some clothes. She said it took some time before he knew what she wanted, like he had to learn.

'He was a bit funny in the head, he couldn't really talk to me, to girls. I don't think he'd ever had a girlfriend.' She stopped suddenly. 'But of course, I don't know. I don't know what he did. At first, he was stupid, then he learned a lot and he made me laugh, he brought me nice things. Life became more comfortable,' she said.

Allen wondered about her mental state, whether he should be doing this interview. It was a bit dubious, he thought, maybe even unethical, not a word he'd ever considered before. It was starting to feel too much like a confessional and he didn't want to be a priest. Twilight was beginning to draw in. He was starting to feel cocooned in the room, as if they had in some way returned to Jennifer's prison, the strange room she was talking about. Time itself was as lost here as it had been there. Through his increasing sleepiness he forced himself to concentrate on her story, to think about what she was saying. He didn't know what was important, what might explain everything.

'He brought me food every day at first, or he left it for me when he disappeared. Tins and that.'

'Disappeared?'

'He did,' she said. 'He went off, sometimes for a week or even more. I don't know where he went, he wouldn't tell me.' He left her with the food and a bucket for a toilet. 'After a few months he got one of them chemical toilets,' she said, 'but it

28

smelled much worse than the bucket.' She made a face. 'It was better though. He didn't like emptying it, see?'

Allen tried to imagine how twelve years could pass in a tiny space, how she had coped with not seeing daylight or talking to any others. He asked how she passed the time.

'He brought me some books. Another man came sometimes and talked to me. Then there was a video machine, and films. I slept a lot; I think it was in the food, something to make me sleep. I liked to be asleep more than awake. When The Prick came to visit I wasn't allowed to talk much, but when the other man came we talked a lot and watched television together.

'He did buy me nice clothes, but sometimes I had to wear the same clothes for a long time, maybe even a year. Sometimes he didn't come to visit me for a long time. I opened tins of food when I wanted to, but I didn't like it.

'I missed my mother and my brother all the time, then in the end I forgot about them. What I mean is, I couldn't really re-member what it was like to see them every day. It was different: my life before the room became like a dream that I could hardly remember. In my room I was safe. I dreamed that my room was on top of a huge tree blowing in the wind and I was a princess who could not be allowed to escape because a prince wanted to marry her, a prince from a tiger kingdom who would eat her up.'

'Do you know why he let you go?' he asked. He had been trying to work out why she was let out, what had triggered her release after all that time.

'Of course,' she said. 'It's our plan. I'm going to be famous. I'm going to be on television, and he's going to watch me. That's what we agreed.'

He wasn't expecting that and now began to wonder where this was going.

'Why does he want to do that?' he asked.

'Because that's how the world works. Because that was what we agreed, when we got married, that he would let me go but I would always be visible, he could always see me.'

'How can he see you?'

'I don't know.' She shrugged. 'He's clever, and I have to go where he can, that's all. That's why I need to be on television.'

'What happens if it doesn't work, if you don't become famous?' he asked.

'It will work. If it doesn't, I'm going back to him.'

'Why?'

'Because I love him,' she said.

There was a sound at the door. When he turned, Jennifer's mother was standing there. 'I think you two should stop now, you'll get Jennifer all tired out. I think we've done enough for today. Would you like a cup of tea?' she asked. He looked at his watch. Two hours had passed in this crowded room. 'No thanks,' he said. He turned back to his interviewee.

'Thanks, Jennifer,' he said. 'That was a good start. I hope it's not been too much for you?'

'It's been lovely,' she said. 'Will you do my book?'

'I would really like to. I'll come back and if we still get on, I think so. We'll need to spend more time together, and you'll need to tell me your story properly. Everything. I'll write it down as we go along, record some of it. How does that sound?'

Her mother interrupted from behind him. 'I'm sure we can arrange something, assuming that man gets a contract,' she said, making clear that today was over.

Allen stood up and stretched his stiff legs.

'Goodbye Jen,' he said.

She looked away, not answering as he left the room.

The people gathered downstairs didn't seem in any hurry to leave. They were settling in for a drinking session. Laughter reverberated around the house. As he left, Jennifer's mother told him he should certainly come back. 'I think she likes you, but let's wait until she's calmed down a bit,' she said. He still wasn't sure whether she really wanted it to happen, but he was determined to write this book.

Walking back to the bus stop, he wondered how he would take it if that were his daughter, if he'd lost her for twelve years. He had a daughter of his own who he hadn't seen for several years, an uncomfortably similar situation, he realised. At least he knew where she was, who she was with. He only had to pick up the phone. She hadn't gone without a trace. Not like Jennifer. But Jennifer had come back. And was threatening to go again. It didn't make much sense. There was worse, he thought. She seemed to have bonded with her captor, unlike most of the stories he was hearing. He couldn't relate it to personal experience, to know the wrench of that sort of loss. He could try and imagine it. Bringing a child into the world, looking after it, learning everything about it day after day, watching it change from a fragile baby, only to lose it to ... to what?

During the journey home his mind churned over the logic, the history, the timings of this event. He tried to relate it to his own knowledge. When she had gone, who might have been around, where she was held. She hadn't given him any clues, not yet. He wondered what the police had asked her, what efforts they were making to find this place. They might not believe her story. Did he? It wasn't really a valid question; her story fitted perfectly well into what he knew about these things, how human beings could be hidden away in the middle of a city without anyone noticing, be broken down. Even friends and family could sometimes pretend to themselves that there was nothing wrong. He'd found it staggering how a partner was party to the predations of their loved one, like Detroux's girlfriend in Belgium, how she'd left two girls to starve to death in his basement while he was in prison. Scared, she said. Human fear, fear of loneliness, love, abuse, control, manipulation – powerful motivators. And Jennifer, maybe she could lead him to whoever had held her: The Prick, as she called him. If he was watching, if they did have a plan. It seemed crazy, he knew, but stranger things did happen. Maybe.

When he got home there was a message from Jenkins. Urgent it said, but when he called him, it wasn't.

'I need feedback. I want the gory details. Is she a deformed hobbit girl?' Jenkins pleaded, but Allen wasn't in a mood to deliver. He was sinking into melancholy, remembering the way she had talked and talked without ever emerging as a functional human. He felt he had to get back to see her again.

Emily was at work and the flat was quiet and cold. He wanted her back, someone to hold on to, to feel human warmth. He'd see her later, after work, but he knew she'd be wrapped up in schoolwork, her mind activated by thirty small children, full of arguments and small progresses. She didn't like his work at the best of times, least of all when she was immersed in the vocal clamour of her class.

He made himself some beans on toast and sat on the sofa with them, running Jennifer's words around in his head. *If it doesn't work, I'm going back to him.*

He uploaded the interview onto the computer and listened to a small part of it. It was so predictable, he decided. And, it was crap. Well, that wasn't fair, she was listless, unable to help him understand what had happened. She wasn't answering anything, just going through the motions. He couldn't blame her, poor thing, she must be fucked up. He wondered if the mother had been lurking on the landing the whole way through. What did she think, that he might assault her? That she might tell him something he shouldn't hear? It might be the only way she could hear about her daughter's missing years. If so, he couldn't blame her. That might be why she'd set up the interview in the first place. What a mess, he thought.

Then for no reason he was swept with a tremor of awful desire for his own child, for another person to look after, to safeguard. And not for the first time, he imagined those who were still locked in dark spaces, and he shuddered.

He picked up the phone and rang Emily's mobile, but got her voicemail.

'Want to come round tonight?' he said to the phone. 'I'll cook.'

Later that night, after they'd eaten and drunk a bottle of wine between them and shortly before they fucked, she asked him how the meeting with Jennifer had gone. He trod carefully around her question. She wasn't a fan of his work and would often take offence at assumptions he made. He was the expert, he researched the subject, but still felt at a disadvantage when questioned by an innocent. After she'd gone to bed, he went back to the book he was reading, *Tutankhamen: The Story of a Tomb*, but he couldn't settle.

There still had been no more emails from the person who had sent the keepens video. That footage was more interesting to him than a hundred Jennifers. It meant that someone was reaching out to him, wanted him to know something; it might be a doorway to a world he had glimpsed but never could enter. Jennifer, on the other hand, was over, released, finished as a story. But who was reaching out, and what did they want to tell him? He checked his account obsessively, wanting to keep the contact live, but for now there was just silence.

The Mile End

A few days later Jennifer's mother rang. He was surprised to hear her sounding so cheerful.

'Hi Julie,' he said. 'Everything alright?'

He shifted the phone to under his chin, held it tight and continued making tea and toast while she talked. He dexterously shifted toast, butter, jam, teabag, mug and milk from place to place and let her ramble on for a while about her family and her lawyer. Finally, she got to the point.

'Jennifer wants to talk to you,' she said. 'She wants to show you something.'

He stopped buttering and put the toast down.

'She might know where she was held,' she said, adding quickly, 'I know that sounds crazy.'

He was tempted but wary. He'd heard that story before. 'Have you told the police?' he said, hoping that she hadn't. He wanted the next part of the puzzle to himself, if there was one. 'Has she said what she knows?'

'She won't let me do anything and she won't tell me anything. She only wants to tell you. She says you should help her find it, the place where she was.'

'What does she mean?'

'If you'll go with her, maybe she can work it out.'

He wondered what this would lead to. Maybe her interment had made her crazy after all. But there was no question that he'd go. There was something unique about her, a confidence he hadn't encountered before. After the call he sat down and thought. He was sure she couldn't know how to find the location. Then he wondered what they would do if they did find it. Was this man, The Prick, sitting in his flat waiting for her to reappear? It didn't seem likely, but what did he know?

'Why not the police?'

'She likes you. I think you've made a friend. And she doesn't like the police, you know that. That's all, really.'

'Should I come now?'

'If you can, please. Can we meet at the tube station at Mile End? Do you know it?'

'Yes,' he said.

'And bring a map. She's scaring me a bit.'

'Give me ninety minutes,' Allen said and put the phone down. He looked for a cab but soon gave up and walked to the tube station and started his journey again.

It took him over an hour but he met them outside the underground station and although it was plain Jennifer's mother wanted to come further, both Allen and Jennifer stared her down. She backed into the tube and disappeared. They walked off around the corner and Jennifer took Allen's arm, looped hers right through and held on tight to him. Maybe we look like a couple, he thought, in dismay.

He'd grabbed a map of London. 'Show me this station, where we are,' she said, so he marked it with a big arrow. She spent a long while looking at the map, turning it round and round as if to orientate something in her head. Then she pointed to a council estate on the Isle of Dogs. Allen knew it vaguely. 'I think if we go there, I can work it out,' she said,

She was a different person to the recalcitrant lump he'd interviewed the other day. She hung on his arm as they walked towards the pendulous droplet of land suspended above the Thames that was for some reason called an island. It wasn't, though it was strangely cut off from the city and encapsulated by the river on three sides and the looming glass towers of the new office blocks on the fourth.

Jenni bloomed in the sunlight and had obviously put some effort into how she looked for their mission, as she called it. He was wearing his usual jeans and hoodie; she was dressed in tights and a short skirt with a denim jacket over a T-shirt that bore a large slogan. Bit dated, he thought, but then what did he expect? He was nervous, she didn't seem so.

'Have you got a girlfriend?' she asked.

He said he did.

'What's she like?'

Allen thought about it. 'She's a teacher. She works with children all day. I guess she's good at it, but I couldn't be – I like to be out and about.'

'What's her name?'

He wasn't sure whether it was a good idea to answer that, but he did. 'Emily.'

'I like that name. And I'd like to be a teacher.'

'And be on television? Anything else you'd like to do?'

It didn't seem she'd been asked this question before.

'When I was in there, I used to think about what I would do when I got free. The Prick used to go on about getting me on the stage and how to get on TV and all that; and how hard I would have to work and how important it all was going to be so I never thought about any other job. Not even about getting married or having children. I don't think I could do anything, I'm not clever enough. I never even finished school.'

'You didn't finish school because you couldn't. That's hardly your fault, right? Didn't you read a lot over the years?'

'I did, I read whatever he brought me, a lot of books, magazines. But I didn't learn much from them.'

She turned towards a newsagent's window filled with trinkets and gaudy magazines.

'Look,' she said. 'Jewellery. That's beautiful.' She stood and stared for a while at the cheap chains and earrings. 'Have you got any money?'

Allen smiled at her. He took her hand. 'Come on then.' Twelve years, he thought. She deserved it. He wondered what Emily would make of this, holding hands with this rather pretty woman in a strange part of town, buying her jewellery. And because the thought had occurred to him, he realised it was a dangerous thought, or that there was danger lurking behind the innocent. He dropped her hand suddenly, but Jennifer didn't notice. She was entranced by the array of glittering objects. She selected a necklace, iridescent glass beads hung on a silver chain, which he paid for.

'It's a present,' he said as they left the shop. 'To say thanks for helping me out.' She smiled at him and he felt even more guilty.

'Come on then,' he said. 'Let's get on with it.'

They approached a busy junction.

'I remember this road,' she said. 'We walked up here, me and The Prick, the last time I saw him.'

She told him how she'd been taken from the room by the man who had kept her locked up for twelve years, how they'd walked up the road to the tube station. She said she'd tried to remember the route, although he would not let her turn around.

Allen walked where she indicated, but it was soon obvious she was lost or confused. He steered her into a coffee shop and they drank lattes.

'I never had anything like this all the time I was captured.' She had taken to calling her kidnap time her capture.

'When he walked me up to the station to abandon me, I looked in shop windows to see reflections. I wanted to see where I'd come from. I saw these tower blocks, the very big ones. I knew we had walked under them and come out on this road.'

She seemed unhappy. He wondered what her relationship with her abductor had become, what all those years meant.

'Should I tell you something, something I know, that I always knew? How I knew where I was? When I was in that place all those years, where I wasn't supposed to know where I was? I could see out. There was a crack in the wall and I could see out. It was a view, you know, I was looking down from high up, like I was in a tower block. I was in a tower block, that's what I mean. That's all I know, I was in a room in a tower block, high up, very high up. I could see the river, sometimes I'd see ships. It was only a little crack, but if I lay on my side I could see out and I could feel the wind through it. Sometimes I lay there all day looking out through my little keyhole. That's what I called it, my little keyhole, because I thought it might get me out of there one day.'

She laughed.

Why would a kidnapper keep her locked up for twelve years and then walk her to the local station and leave her there?

'So where was this tower?'

'I don't know. How would I know?' The petulant teenager again. 'But I might be able to work it out. He told me that there were others who wanted me, who would take me away.'

'Do you think that was true?' said Allen.

'Yes, it is. I met them,' she said. 'I went to places with him. He took me to see people. We planned it together, it was part of the plan, to get famous, so I could look after him.'

Now Allen was confused.

'What the fuck are you talking about?'

Her face fell. She looked up at him like a small child. 'I'm sorry,' he said. 'I don't know what you mean.'

'You shouldn't talk to me like that,' she said. 'You must say sorry.'

'Yes, of course. I'm sorry,' he said. 'But what did he take you to? What did you do?'

'To auditions, of course. The Prick said if I could get onto telly he would let me go, because then he'd know where I was. He taught me to sing, and dance, and things like that.'

'You went and met people for acting parts?' He was incredulous. 'What happened?'

'I never got any parts,' she said, deflating again. 'It was because they were jealous of me. That's what he said. Then he told me we had a different plan and we never went out again. That was when he said he'd let me go if I promised to do our plan.'

'And did you?'

'What?' she said.

'Did you promise to keep to his plan?'

She looked at him, wide-eyed. 'Of course, I did,' she said. 'That's how I got out.'

She was a different person today, out in the open. No longer the lumpen girl-child that he had tried to interview in that hot room, she seemed to blossom in the outdoors, on the London street. Lorries roared past and he found it hard to catch some of what she said. He leaned closer in, it seemed important to follow as she talked. They seemed to be drifting around with little idea of direction, but maybe that was necessary, he decided. She reached out and held his hand for a while. He looked around.

'Do you recognise anything?'

'Let's go to the towers. I could see a bit of them from my room, through a gap he didn't know was there. It was my sunshine hole. I looked out for hours when he wasn't there and I thought about all the people working in those buildings.'

They crossed onto the Isle of Dogs. He'd hung out here a long time ago, before the tower blocks came and swept away the connection between the Dogs and the rest of London. Those monstrous blocks, built to house the banks of the world, were coming fully into view as they strode south. I'd rather be at home writing, he thought.

The last coffee they'd had was now a distant memory and Allen's feet were sore. Jennifer didn't seem bothered in the slightest, she was in some sort of dream world. She'd navigated in a zig-zag fashion, now running off down this street, now doglegging back in the opposite direction. He'd begun to wonder whether there actually was a destination, whether she was just playing games with him. But in the end, it became clear that they were headed in a specific direction, that she had the scent of where she wanted to go. It just took a long time to get there.

They traversed the towers of the northern Isle, cutting through a zone that was not designed for pedestrian foot traffic.

'When I first came to London,' he said, 'this was almost an abandoned zone. People did live here, of course, but they lived in a sort of different country. There was one road on to the island at each side. Everything was old-fashioned, but there was a sort of pride that the people here had. I think it's all gone now, since they built a new city on the Thames.'

She looked at him. 'I didn't know it was an island.'

'It's not, not really. But it's always been called one, the Isle of Dogs.'

After that there was a long period of silent walking. They dipped into the bowels of the skyscrapers and ended up walking through a dark and dangerous tunnel. Jennifer became tense and jittery in the underground passageway and walked faster and faster until he was striding to keep up. Finally, they emerged on the south side of the towers. The sun was up, raised railways hung in the air on all sides. Down below, on what seemed like mainly abandoned ground, there were building sites, endless arrays of housing, all the same. Ahead of them against the sky stood two or three tower blocks, tiny in comparison to what they had just travelled under, the remains of social housing projects from the sixties and seventies.

Jennifer stood and stared at these buildings.

'That's it,' she said. 'One of those.'

She started to shake and Allen took hold of her shoulders. He could feel the tremors running through her body.

'Scared?' he asked.

'No,' she said.

Tired and thirsty, they arrived at the foot of a twenty-story residential block. They approached the building through grey dusty streets lined with small red-brick buildings sitting in the shadow of a line of four towers like a parody of executive housing. Some of the houses had neat, tidy gardens filled with flowers, others contained nothing but rusting household goods, piles of sodden newspapers, rolled up carpets or half-disassembled scooters, long abandoned. Some even had both.

Finally, they stopped walking and she craned her neck to look up, then turned and stared at a small cluster of shabby housing towers which looked grey and miserable in the shadow of the huge development. She pointed at them. 'That's where I was, up there, in the front one.'

'This one?' he said.

'Must be. I could see this building closest through my spy hole, I think we're about in the right place.'

She took his hand forcefully and, with renewed energy, led him away from the office blocks into the more human-scaled world of the Isle of Dogs itself. Soon the contemporary road layout and commercial mix was behind them and they were skirting a collection of council housing estates and miserable shopping streets. The remains of industry clustered along the riverside but people had hung on here, long after the dockside work had gone and the land been gifted to international commerce. They hung on because there was really nowhere else to go and because there was tradition and family in the area. The residential towers were tiny in comparison to the vast commercial monoliths they had recently passed below. He could see how different it was here but, Allen thought, although it was grubby and worn out, it was also more human. It was a real place where people lived out their lives, even if those lives were secret and totally hidden from the world.

Eventually they made their way to the nearest tower. Above the door a sign said Quarterdeck House. They looked at the ramped entranceway, the barriers guiding tenants and visitors towards heavy glass and dark wood doors. An array of regimented buttons greeted them on an aluminium box next to the door. The door itself was locked. He tried buzzing a few random flats. On the third press a voice answered.

'Hello.'

'Hello. Could you let me in, please?'

'Fuckrightoff.'

He took that as a no. Jennifer had wandered off. He saw her disappear around the corner.

'Jen,' he shouted. 'Don't go off.'

He was nervous, this was new territory. The place was threatening. He wasn't sure whether he believed her in the slightest, but she claimed to recognise the building. Could it be that she'd been held high up in this tower for years, in a room with boarded windows? He felt she was far too calm for someone who was approaching her own prison and it had occurred to him that if this was the place then they might meet her captor at any moment. He'd been writing about the kidnapping underworld for a few years but he'd never actually met any of them. He'd been to visit various holding sites before but he'd certainly never imagined taking a victim back into the place of incarceration.

A police car cruised slowly past the building. He watched it slow at the end of the short street and then turn the corner. He knew it was not there because of him, but still it frightened rather than reassured him. His police contacts had warned him about getting involved. He had put this down to jealousy, that they'd failed to make headway with her when they had the chance. That copper, Herman, had the press on his back and although the police would be happy to use his knowledge of the underworld to get a result, he knew there'd be trouble as soon as they found out he was doing his own footwork.

Then he realised that Jennifer hadn't reappeared around the corner. Allen vaulted the handrail and quickly ran to the corner of the building, then around it. He looked out across an empty concrete yard but she was nowhere in sight. There were no people there at all, only a couple of television sets that had clearly been jettisoned from a great height. He crossed the open expanse, wary of getting the third set on his head, and scanned the area. Eventually he saw her, sitting on a low wall a few hundred feet back from the building, staring up at the roof of the building, shielding her eyes against the sun with her hand.

He tilted his own head back and looked up to see where she was looking. The balconies rose in front of him like an aggregate cliff. Seagulls wheeled and cawed around the edifice. Clearly some balconies were nesting sites, many others were netted against their presence. He tried to imagine who lived in the various flats. Some were immaculate and some, like the gardens of the houses along the road, were loaded with junk. Allen wondered what it was like to live up in the sky. He'd never lived any higher than the second floor of a house, and as he'd not known anyone who lived in such a building, he had no experience of vertical streets.

On the concrete pillars at the base of the tower, inscriptions read *Fuck You Jerry* and *Loves Pam and Dog* along with various symbols, hearts and genitals in a cartoon fashion. The craze for artistic graffiti had not yet reached the more remote estates on the Isle of Dogs. This was human emotion written in spray paint, not art from educated vandals.

'Jen,' he shouted at her back. Slowly she stood up and walked across to him. Rubbish caught in a down draft caused by the tower created an unpleasant vortex at the base. Crips packets and carrier bags were picked up and spun in the air and against his legs. Allen pressed his fingers against his eyelids to protect them from a stinging barrage of tiny whirling scraps borne in the cloud of dust. He held his mouth tightly shut. Jennifer ran through the middle of the storm and grabbed hold of him. 'Help,' she laughed, spinning him around with the airborne junk. He was amazed at her lack of fear.

She linked her arm through his, turned and walked him back to the entrance. They waited impatiently until an old lady slowly exited from the building, giving them a chance to enter under the guise of assisting her. 'Thanks,' they said in unison. She gave them a dirty look as they held the door open and walked in. The lobby was grey: grey tiled floor, grey eggshell walls, grey acoustic ceiling tiles and grey lift doors. The early evening light was fading now, adding to the monotone colour scheme of the building. They crossed over to the lifts. Allen saw they had tape stretched in front of them and a small handwritten sign stuck to the doors: *Not working, sorry, engineer on his way.* Underneath this somebody had drawn a penis and written, *Wanker, 3 days now, fix the foking lifts.*

43

He looked across to the staircase to the right of the lifts. It would be a long climb. He motioned with his head towards the stairs.

'How far up?'

Jennifer whined. 'Aww, I don't want to climb them.'

'Let's go then,' he said.

'I don't want to go.'

'We don't have much choice. The lift's fucked.'

He didn't understand why she had wanted to come here and he certainly didn't think it was much of an idea to go to the top of the building, but he was drawn on by her insistence. He wondered if he was actually scared of what they might find. It was his promise to Jenkins and his curiosity that kept him here. Mostly curiosity. He didn't expect to find anything at the top, he didn't even believe this could be the right building, or that she was telling the truth, or even, if it came to it, that much of her story was true. Wherever she'd been held, up, down or fucking sideways, and quite what they were doing at this tower block, suddenly all seemed like a fool's errand.

An internal fear gripped him, but he pushed it so far away that he felt ordinary again, bored even.

It was like one of those hypnosis shows where people were put under the influence and then regressed to a previous life. They would answer questions and come up with increasingly tortured explanations of what they did in a past incarnation without ever having to answer difficult questions or explain how it was they came to be reborn. With Jennifer it was as if she was recounting a previous life that was entertaining but in which he really could have no belief at all. He did believe that she'd been held against her will – he knew that there were people who could, and would, abduct girls purely to hold them for years – but he suspected that a lot more had gone on in the years she was missing. A lot more than she was admitting to. However, he was prepared to leave it for now. His professional life depended on this moment and what it might reveal. He had to keep all his antennae working.

She looked at the lift again and shook her head. 'I know the lift's fucked; it was always fucked.'

'So, do we climb, or go?'

'Let's climb it, Allen.' Suddenly she was climbing the first steps, almost running up.

He stood there for a few more moments, frozen, as she moved faster. He looked up at the lift, at the stairs, still hesitating for some reason to start the climb in earnest. He stared at her, letting her work through whatever was bothering her.

Then, from above him she shouted, 'No, not up. Down. It always goes down.'

She took the initiative, walked to the stairwell and disappeared. He jumped out of his daydream and ran after her.

It took him a moment to get to the corner but she was gone again. He looked into the gloom. The stairs here went down as well as up. Which way had she gone, up or down? What had she shouted? He hesitated for a moment in fearful indecision, and then two at a time he leapt down into the dark before realising that there were only six steps and that he was going to hit the bottom at high speed. He hit the dirty concrete floor and skidded across it, coming to a halt against a locked, rusty metal fire door. There was no sign of her. He called out and waited a moment. Standing up, he shouted for her again, the fear tightening in his chest. Jennifer. Jennifer. Jennifer. But there was no reply. He ran back up the steps and looked around, then as fast as he could, down to the lobby and out through the doors. He ran round the entire building, then stopped to catch his breath. He tried to think seriously about where she could have gone. By logic she must be right here somewhere, or in the lobby or behind a concrete pillar or standing by the lift. But she was nowhere. He stepped back and tilted his head to look up at the tower block which seemed to stretch forever up into the grey sky. As he backed away from it, more and more windows came into view, some neat and tidy, some covered in grey cardboard or rotting net curtains. Every flat looked different, every flat could contain The Prick – or Jennifer. She was gone and she was his responsibility. Now he felt a rising panic in his stomach.

'Fuck, fuck, fuck, fuck,' he muttered to himself. I've lost her. I've taken her away from her family, back to the most dangerous place in the world and I've fucking gone and lost her. He ran back to the building and banged on the front door which returned a booming echo but would not shift. Then a tiny ageing woman with a shopping trolley pushed the door open from the inside and Allen almost fell back into the lobby.

Suddenly, unexpectedly, he started to cry. He stood motionless while tears ran down his face. and as he sobbed, he wailed Jennifer, Jennifer.

And then, suddenly, she was standing there, looking at him, all innocence in her childish skirt and the jewellery he'd bought her earlier that day.

'Why are you crying?' she said.

The sobbing stopped immediately and Allen wiped his eyes with the back of his hand.

'Where the fuck have you been?'

His anger came from fear, but it had a bad effect on Jennifer. She shrank back away from him. Then, in a whisper she asked to go home.

Invitation

He took two bottles of wine home with him that evening as a peace offering to Emily.

'That copper has been round again,' she told him, before he'd even put them down.

'Herman?'

'He gave me an earful,' she said. 'They don't like your *Silence of the Lambs* stuff and they're not happy with your unhelpful attitude. You know you're going to be in deep shit at this rate.'

'There's nothing they can do, and they know there's nothing I've done. They're just pissed off with me because they think I know more than them. I don't, actually. Not yet. Well, maybe one thing – the girl might know where it all happened, where she was held.'

'How could she know that?'

'She doesn't want to tell us, but she's been out and about with him. In fact, I think she's withholding information about their whole life together. Something strange went on. What do you think – she told me she'd been to auditions, to get on telly. Is that possible?'

Emily grimaced. She wanted to allow a human connection to this poor kid, but still she didn't want to hear about Allen's world.

'Sounds like big trouble to me,' she said. 'You can't just go running about town with girls who've been abducted for years, who might be on the edge of cuckoo land – and who the police must surely be watching closely.'

'I know, but she's my source. I'm supposed to be writing her book, I've got to get something out of her—poor thing. She was only a teenager when he took her.'

'Who? Who took her?'

'This guy. She calls him the Prick. Of course, she knows a lot more than she's letting on. She doesn't want to tell the police everything. She doesn't even want to tell me, not really.'

'What's the point then?'

'The point is – I'm not sure. But she's got some sort of plan, maybe his plan, that they worked out between them. She won't tell the coppers because, quite honestly, she's had enough big guys shouting at her to last a lifetime and they'll just get in her way. She's got some crazy scheme about getting on television, and ending up famous, and that's how he'll know.'

'Know what?' said Emily.

'Know that she kept her side of the bargain. Look, it sounds insane, it is insane. She said this guy, the Prick, who took her, he's been training her for the stage. Oh, I know, it's funny. It's funny, until you hear it from her, then it's not so funny.'

'What does she do? I mean, what can she do to get famous?'

'She's the kid who disappeared for years. Everyone already wants to know what happened, she doesn't have to do much. And she's smart. You should hear her tell her story.'

'Brought a tear to your eye, I suppose.'

'It did actually. Well, you weren't there, you don't know. I mean, I'm not sure anybody will take her seriously, but the press will love it. He taught her everything, been practising for years. Anyway, I'm going to write her book.'

He sat back in triumph. Emily looked at him in amazement.

'So, what have you been doing today?'

'We went to look for her place, where she's been all these years. She took me to a tower block. We almost found where she's been. Almost. I think.'

'I think you should go to the police.'

'And lose the whole story? There's a copper, he wants me, me and Jenkins, out of the case.'

'Well, what can they do? What's the worst that can happen?' Emily said.

'They might take her away, away from her mum. Put her in a home.' He was grasping at straws now 'With what she's been through they might as well put her back in a hole in the ground.'

Emily had heard this rant before. 'Well, what next?' she asked.

'Well. First, why was she let go? That's a good question, a good place to start. Twelve years is a long time to hang on to someone, and then you just walk them to the corner and say bye-bye. And another thing, I think she knows where she was and if that's true it doesn't make any sense. There were other men who looked after her when The Prick was away. Looked after her. It's like an organised gang and they network like child abusers, but maybe they're not paedophiles. And they're not murderers. They don't murder. They just snatch and keep, know what I mean?'

Any warmth seemed to have been extracted from the room and Emily shivered.

'Then go to the police.'

'I'm not taking this to the coppers. I'm sure I know more than they do now and it's my story.' He realised he sounded petulant. 'Even if I had something concrete to tell them, they wouldn't listen to me, and anyway, I'd be cutting my own throat, giving my best story away. I know a bit of what's going on and I'm not doing their job for them. They've got their own theories and they are dead wrong.'

Despite the seeming enthusiasm of Jennifer's mother, Allen found it impossible to arrange another meeting. There was a string of excuses, then she evaded his phone calls. After a while he realised that there wasn't really going to be a book, at least not if the mother had anything to do with it. He gave in and wrote up what he had for the magazine. *A day in the life of Jennifer Ransome.* He felt some guilt in using their discussions, but something had to be done with the material – it was too interesting to leave sitting in the laptop. He kept the most perplexing details to himself, talk of the man who had held her and Jennifer's belief that she knew where she had been kept. He still held out a slight belief that she would come back to him with more.

Jenkins was not ecstatic. Great article, he said, pity to lose the book. 'I'll work on it, promise.'

Allen continued to wonder about the woman he'd talked to, the girl that she had been and the man who'd kept her all those years, The Prick, and her dreams of fame. Fame for nothing, the modern world, that was what it all came to. Locked up for a lifetime, all it gave you was the idea of a ticket onto television. Maybe she deserved it, he thought.

As expected, the police were very unhappy and, under the command of Pete Herman they descended on the Ransome house and tried to intimidate the family. The family were ready with their lawyer and the press and fought against it, hard. They'd become settled in the big house and didn't want to be thrown out. Allen saw the horror of inflicting this sort of treatment on such a vulnerable person, but it was no longer his story. He'd trodden on what the police regarded as their own inviolate territory and he had little choice but to back far off. Herman took a shot at Jenkins, threatening his business. 'I'll raid you, take everything you've got for evidence and screw you to the floor,' he said.

'It's all there in print,' Jenkins said. 'Help yourself.'

'Fuck you, we'll get a court order,' Herman said. 'We're well within our rights. It's you that is walking on thin ice, how fucking dare you go in there and pump that poor girl for information—and then splash it all over the country? You better watch your back.'

Irate policemen were one thing, but London itself started to bug Allen now. The weather, which had been sunny in a clear, spring-like fashion, had now turned wet. Every time he went out it drizzled on him, the rain running off his leather coat into the pockets, making everything wet and driving him crazy. He cursed the dampness and waited for spring to return. He had another problem, a lack of work. Usually a new job turned up every few weeks, just enough to keep him going. In between writing he emailed around and wrote up story ideas. He tried to start up again on his own book idea, *Lost, buried, abandoned: A history of the taken children* but the proposal was nowhere near finished. He picked at it but he just couldn't get Jennifer's story out of his head.

What he had suspected at the start, what he'd caught various glimpses of over a few years of talking to scum and writing up the shadowy world they knew about, was slowly coming into view. He knew that across Europe, all across the world, people rotted in cellars. Not a lot, but enough. They were the taken, the missing of the earth. Any trawl of the local or national press would turn up stories of the missing. The default view of the police, and of their families, was that they were most likely dead. No matter what circumstances they disappeared in, they never used their credit cards or bank accounts. They didn't contact friends or lovers. They didn't turn up in casualty wards or seeking dental treatment. All contact with the modern world ceased. It was reasonable to assume that they were dead and buried in some shallow grave.

A few of them would escape, many of them die. Some of them raped daily and existed on an appalling diet of whatever the captors would give them or could smuggle for them. Other takers did nothing with their prey beyond locking them in the dark and keeping them there. Some were ill-educated and poor, but others were educated and affluent. There seemed to be no logic to the process, no discernible pattern to explain who would catch and keep their prey and who would be killers. There were no statistics, just the dark secrets, people growing whiter by the day, not knowing what day or season it is, their flesh turning to jelly as they live out their lives, long or short, at the mercy of their keepers. Some lived in base abject misery in damp, cramped boxes, others in palatial luxury in custom-built mansions underground, living a life of pretended splendour more squalid than the worst imprisonment, the deepest wet cellar. No matter what circumstances were constructed for these poor unfortunates, they lived out lives of the utmost banality in conditions that would be described as beyond human imagining, were it were not for the fact that humans had very much imagined them into being.

A week later, while he mucked about with a story that was already overdue, a response came, from the internet, as he had known it would.

He liked these moments, when a gap in his attention ensured there would be something to read. People said you could get addicted to email, to the internet, and he felt sure he was addicted on some level. He found it hard not to check his post every few minutes, no matter what he was doing. When something had taken him away from his workroom for a while, he felt an honest pleasure at getting back to check the email.

did you like the viddy i have something for you, if you are still interested and are ready to travel? you are interested in our keepens i believe? i have a proposal, I think. we met once, a long time back in Lartin, you left me there, you lucky bastard.

you've made a name for yourself alright, I've been following your career, you've been writing about me ha ha. I can give you some good shit on your subject, real stories, not the made-up crap most people spout, ha, ha.

i can show you some of our keepens, it can be arranged i think you'll find things are bit different to what you might imagine.

email me back but don't go spouting your mouth off or the door will close so quickly you will feel like a keepen yourself
as always, your friend

The email system it was sent from had stripped all identity from the sender. The message remained anonymous with no clues to the origin. It could be local, could be the other side of the world. From the language he guessed Eastern Europe, but he really had nothing to go on, just a hunch.

Then, thinking again about the video that had come and gone, he realised that the person who placed it on YouTube must have been sitting at their computer waiting for him to take a look at it. And once they'd seen him arrive and view the material, they removed the video.

They knew that one look would be enough for him, which meant they knew who and what he was. It was an offer, an invitation.

He had been chasing this world for a long time, and it had made him infamous and feared in certain small circles. Infamous among the public and publishers who loved the cruelty and gore of his stories, but hated his closeness to the perpetrators. Feared among the smaller circles of the perpetrators and the traffickers who operated in the darkness and to whom any light was bad news.

While slowly learning the byways of the fast-growing trafficking business over the preceding ten years, Allen had identified and slowly drawn out another scenario – the holding and keeping of the human cargos that the traders dealt in. And beyond that he had heard stories, rumours and whispers of a deeper layer of horror – those who held and kept captives not for days or weeks as part of a trade, but for years as part of a personal ambition. They were the Keepers and the people they held became keepens over time. Not the keepens of storybook and legend, but the undead, existing underground in cages and cellars for decades. The lost, assumed dead, who were kept alive in the dark.

He went back to his email.

Thank you for your video. I am interested. What do you offer? Allen

He clicked send and waited.

Later.

I think you do know this, a group of people who help each other, who support the network. They creating keepens. My

53

friend has one. Yes, Allen, he has one, held deep down there. Others have them too. You should see this place, it's a basement of families in the dark.

You know, a lot of people are held in different places, under the ground. I can introduce you, if you want, take you there. If you are interested in a visit to see this once and for all come to visit us, then maybe you will understand, you will feel the power.

Over the rest of that day, alone in his flat, Allen carried on an email conversation with an unknown person at the other end. He didn't stray far from the screen, checking and rechecking for new responses. His heart raced every time a new email arrived.

Finally.

- You'll have to be my friend. You'll have to be one of us. I can't take you as a journalist, it's too dangerous.

If I can, I'll get you down to visit one. But you won't know where it is. Maybe a blindfold, a car journey. I'm not sure.

They are my friends.

I wouldn't go to the police, not with my background.

-Why are you doing this? asked Allen in reply. What do you want?

-Come and meet me. Then we can talk said the friend.

-Come and talk? Where? asked Allen.

-Belgrade.

- Who are you? But this time there was no reply.

Allen read the exchange again a couple of times and then picked up the phone to Jenkins.

'I think I have a story here,' he said. 'Any chance you could send me to Belgrade? If this is real it's a big story.'

'If?' asked Jenkins.

'Oh, it's real alright. Just, well, sometimes people exaggerate. And sometimes they don't.'

Jenkins haggled, but within twenty minutes it was agreed. Allen emailed back.

-I'm coming. Make arrangements. I'll get the bus from London.

He emailed Emily at her work.

Em, I'm going to Belgrade for a while. I've got a new contact, think it's serious. I think it's the big one. Back soonest, love you.

He knew she hated it and would hate this more than most but he was on a roll.

I'm doing this for you, he thought.

And then straight back came the reply.

Please don't go, I'm scared for you. Don't go on your own. I don't think I can handle it.

I love you, he thought. But I must go.

Once he was sure he was going, that it was as real as it could be, he stood up, crossed the room and knelt in front of a small cabinet. Reaching underneath it with an extended hand and stretched wrist, he felt for his quarry. It had been there a long time, wrapped in clingfilm and attached to the underside of the cabinet with blue tac. He detached it carefully and drew it out, then carried it back to the desk.

He sat down and considered his prize. Like a boy with a favoured treasure, he held his secret which denoted the depths to which he would descend and which had to be kept from the world.

He pulled at the film, stretching and tearing the covering until an envelope was released. He gingerly pulled out a photograph. It was a picture of a young woman holding a baby. Next to them stood a small child. The picture had been taken with a flash; the eyes ~~are~~ reddened as if they are a devil family. The background is a darkened room, no furniture, rough grey walls. The ceiling is low. She is not smiling and has a very pallid, very white face, hair flattened to her skull. She stares at whoever holds the camera with the look of quarry as the hunt approaches its end, a thousand-yard stare. The child is stony-faced. The baby is held tight to the woman's chest.

In the background, almost obscured in the darkness, is a wooden chair and a small wooden table with a bucket and a shoebox on it. There is also the edge of an inflatable child's castle. He has spent dozens of hours poring over this photo. It is his one true relic.

He turns the photo over.

On the back, in biro, was written in an educated and con-trolled hand, *My keepen family. 2002*

On it is written with a childish hand. *Roger? Maybe long term. europe, uk, club? 2001 LM mine*

Stuck to the back with Sellotape is a passport photo of the head and shoulders of a smirking young man with thick red hair, wearing a shirt and tie and a tweed jacket.

Bosnia 1992

A long, straggling column of women and children made its way slowly through the woods in deep shadow. Although the late autumn sun shone on the tops of the trees and occasionally dipped through to the ground, the walkers could only feel cold on their heads and shoulders. They carried possessions wrapped in blankets. Some limped or staggered, supported by their children or family members. They did not talk. As they drew closer it was clear that many bore wounds from bullets or shrapnel, or the cut of a spade or club. Even the children were not spared, many bore wounds. All had closed-down, expressionless faces.

They had been evicted from ancient family villages and hamlets by Arkan's fighters, a fearsome crew of Serbs who had descended, heavily armed, on their countryside. The path that they took had been trodden already by many of their compatriots. Although aware of the gathering storm, they had been living as their parents and grandparents had done, quietly on their small family farms or in villages where they were neither noticed nor commented upon. As war came, they hid themselves away and waited for the fighters to pass through the valleys on their way to distant battles. What they found, however, was that the war was not distant and the fighters did not want to pass through their villages. The campaign started with bloody murder inflicted at random by small groups of outsiders who came carrying guns and knives and garrotting wires. The men were quickly and efficiently separated from the rest of the community. Those who offered any resistance or who even looked into the eyes of these incomers were swiftly and brutally murdered with extreme violence. No shred of pity was offered by these thugs. They brutalised fathers, mothers, grandparents and babies in front of their families.

Men who had not managed to flee into the woods were rounded up and forced onto buses. The posse of northerners whooped and hollered and broke into the village bar. They swiftly drank the contents and set the building ablaze. The streets filled up with corpses scattered in doorways. A United Nations armoured vehicle entered the street from the north and proceeded slowly and inelegantly down the main road. Although the villagers expected it to stop, for the smartly dressed soldier who manned the machine gun in the turret to turn his firepower on the brutes, to effect a rescue, the armoured car just continued through the village and disappeared at the other end. This visitation sent the now drunken rabble into further paroxysms of Dionysian frenzy and they started to pick off the younger women, taking them away from their families and into a large barn beside the road. By the time night fell, the children had long since stopped crying and subsided into empty, hollow-eyed silence. The villagers knew what was expected of them and they swiftly packed up anything that remained in the way of food and clothing and took to the hills, a community scratched out and forced into a march at a moment's notice.

They slept in those hills, morbidly afraid to descend to the towns despite the freezing weather. They listened to the sound of artillery, of bombardment and churning truck wheels as village after village, town after town was efficiently cauterised and emptied. This was conquest; and safety, they knew, lay to the south. All were traumatised, some more than others. As they reached the top of a steep incline and started down yet another hill, into yet another small valley, they noticed that there were Western journalists, photographers, watching them pass. To their right, hanging part-way up a small tree, the body of a young woman. Dressed in a red jersey and white stained skirt, she had hanged herself with her own belt. The passersby took no notice, but the journalists were fascinated and took photo after photo as the remnants of the northern villages passed by oblivious, wall-eyed and deep in their own thoughts of survival.

They made their way down and, for a change and because they are exhausted, some of them took to the road to cross to the further slopes over which they needed to climb on their journey to safety, kept in motion only by the thought that over the next hill, in the next valley, there might be a safe space, a sanctuary where they could stop and rest. Beyond that they had no thoughts.

While they are moving slowly and painfully along this road, a large white Mercedes car appears and pulls up slowly along-side the women at the back of the convoy. Fearing for their lives, they motion the car forward. It moves again along the line and draws up beside a small group, two young women, one grandmother and one a young girl. They look unwillingly into the car whose windows are now wound up tight. The men inside are dressed in civilian clothing, not the army fatigues with which they have become familiar and of which they are in mortal fear. A man in the back seat holds a gun, a small machine pistol. But he also holds food and money; a ham, bread, cheeses, biscuits. The women look into the car in won-der and the man motions to the girl. We don't know her, they say, she was on the hills alone, her parents are … But they tail off here because they don't know who the parents are and to speculate on where they are is to open a box that is being held firmly closed by force of will throughout the group. She's not ours, they say, aware that they are crossing a line that ought not to be crossed, but somehow now broken by events.

The girl looks up, she has learned recently that nobody is to be trusted, but she also notices the bread, the cheese, and that the men do not wear the battle fatigues that clothed those who started this nightmare. She smiles sweetly at the man holding the food. He gestures to her, come on here. He opens the door and invites her to hop in beside him. The interior of the car is inviting, clean, quiet. Her feet are sore, bloody, bruised. Her shoes are worn through, wet and cold. The driver looks around. He reminds her briefly of her father, or so she tells herself, of papa who she has not seen for two weeks. It is not so much a struggle as a negotiation and when the first man breaks off a hunk of bread and holds it out to her she is won over and leaps into the car. The two women in the group hold fast to the car door and hold out their hands for their prize. Bread, ham, cheese and wine is handed over quickly, then the man gestures with his gun and the old fear returns. The women step away from the car and the door is slammed. The driver guns the idling motor and, with a squeal of tyre rubber, the German automobile accelerates along the road and disappears into the mist.

'And what was her name?' asks the first woman.

'Poor lamb, I have no idea,' says the second, staring at the bread and ham she now holds in her hands.

Allen

Entering the underground that morning, Allen had felt the familiar pang of desire as he descended deep into the station. He felt the heat rise as the endless escalator took him deeper and deeper. He always wondered why it got so hot below ground. It wasn't as if they were getting anywhere near the core of the earth, he knew that. But there was heat from somewhere. He reasoned to himself that it should get cooler as he went deeper. But it always got hotter, even in the middle of winter.

He took hold of Emily's hand and they walked down the platform and waited for a train heading south. Eventually it arrived and they boarded and took seats facing each other. Emily fussed with magazines and newspapers in her bag, eventually upending them over the carriage floor. He snapped at her, then, noting the look on her face, took it back. She was upset, which always made her clumsy.

He amused himself by taking pictures of doorways he passed along the platform and between levels, locked doorways. Sealed entrances. No explanation. The occasional small sterile sign signifying nothing. There must be a network of tunnels and corridors and rooms, extending around and below the stations themselves. He liked his mobile phone for this purpose: it took good photos in the gloomy depths. He had a huge collection stored online that he shared with other enthusiasts.

A fragment from a film he'd seen years back popped into his mind. He couldn't remember the name of it, but he recalled a man, chased into the subway and pursued onto the platform. Trapped by an enemy at each end, he suddenly dropped to the rails and found his way into a subterranean space under the station where he met a crew of crazies. What was that film, he wondered?

He had read of people living in the tunnels and in the shafts and in the sewers. It seemed that this happened in other countries, not here in London. More like a New York thing. We were a little too uptight here, and there really didn't seem to be many spare tunnels. Not that he'd really ever looked. Well, not in the railway tunnels. He made a mental note to pay more attention to the tunnels.

'Dreaming?' asked Emily.

He snapped back to the present. 'Nothing, really.' But she could feel the tension inside him.

Now the train arrived at their station and, as the doors opened, they climbed out of the train and found their way through the maze of tunnels and staircases to the exit. They emerged and navigated through the huge Victorian station, exiting and turning towards the bus station.

Halfway along the road, Emily suddenly stopped and, pulling him back to her, said, 'I don't want you to go. This doesn't feel good.'

'I have to go,' he said. 'You know that. I have to go. I'm on my mobile, it won't stop working. Ring me anytime.'

She was crying.

'I thought you understood,' he said. 'This is my work. This could be big. I'll be back in a week.'

'I understand, but I don't understand,' she retorted. 'I do. I did. I thought I did. Now I'm scared.'

I'm scared too, he thought. 'There's no problem. I'll be back in a week. You can call me anytime. I've waited a long time for this, you know that.'

She looked into his eyes and held tightly on to him.

'Be careful out there. They're all sickos,' she said.

'Don't be daft. They're just people. Normal people, most of them.'

'Not who you're going to see,' she said. 'I read it in *The Express*. Gangsters. Criminal capital of Europe. It's a hangover from the communists – they all became criminals. They're wicked.'

'Yeah, they're aliens in disguise,' he said to shut her up, but it didn't, and he had quickly felt guilty at his glib sarcasm. She's scared for me, he thought.

'Come back soon,' she said. 'I'm not happy on my own.'

He had touched her hair softly.

'I just wish you weren't going,' she said. 'I hate it when you go off and leave me alone.' She kissed his lips and turned quickly away.

He watched her walk back up the street, then he turned back to his own thoughts and immediately forgot her. He walked down to the bus station, pulling his ticket out as he strode.

Emily

After Allen left, Emily found she was relieved to get a day without either him or her class of children. She needed to escape from London for a while and, as it was half term, she had a week to hide away. Her mother still occupied the family house she'd grown up in, nestled in the London suburbs. The houses there were solid and well built and the gardens long and languid. Her room was always waiting for her and, although she found it contained reminders of her somewhat mimsy teens, she could hide there, sleep all she wanted, drink tea, gossip with her mother and catch up with a friend or two. That usually reminded her of just how far she'd come, how her escape, while not complete, was reasonable. She had momentum, even if her trajectory wasn't perfect.

She drove south, straight through the centre of town, and reached Croydon in about an hour. A cluster of office blocks surrounded by endless roads; it was not her idea of London. She surprised her mother as she got back from yoga.

'What about Allen?' she was asked quickly. Her mother, as always, was both nervous that it might be over and secretly hoping it was.

'He's away, working.'

'Work?' said her mother. 'That's what he calls it?'

To Emily, things happened within a structure provided by bureaucracy. If you kept within the spirit and letter of their rules, you were allowed to continue to operate. If you upset them, in any way, they came down on you fast but politely. You knew where you were with her job, unlike the freelance stuff that Allen did. He never knew from one week to the next if he would be working or where he'd be working.

'Yes,' she said. 'It's his work, and he's good at it.'

Allen, she thought, was the muscular Christian type, without the Christ bit. He was ex-army with a numinous desire to fix everything through the correct application of the correct kit. Or, if not the correct kit, then the appropriate firepower.

Teaching in a large primary school on the borders of Islington and Camden was grinding her down. It wasn't the worst school, even in the borough, but it had its share of hard characters. Although they were young, some children had experienced terrible things and would taunt their teachers with their knowledge, especially the younger and female staff. She was adept at brushing off the revelations and indeed felt some pity for the twisted and broken children among them, but every now and again she needed to escape. Allen's line of work didn't help. No matter how much she tried to avoid knowing anything of his research, he also needed to unburden himself sometimes. They had similarities, crossovers, she acknowledged, although he chased his demons while she was victim to hers.

She wasn't even sure how she had ended up as a teacher, and it bugged her. She'd never wanted to be one. It had, maybe, started with a stupid affair at the end of her school days, something she would not have allowed when a few years older, but it tainted the end of her education. Escape was what it had been about, and then, when it finished messily, the chance to move anywhere appealed. In the long summer after graduating, still adrift, she signed up for almost the first thing she thought of, which was teacher training. At the time she didn't even know quite what that meant, but now she did – endless days stuck in a smelly room with thirty incontinent children.

'He's a good guy,' she assured her mother. 'He writes what he has to. You know that. Crime and stuff. If he has to go, he has to go. I don't mind.'

She realised her mother put all her lovers in the same club. 'It's mysterious, that he has to keep gallivanting around the world without you. He'll not come back one time, you mark my words,' she said.

Emily smiled to herself. How ludicrous that was.

The arrival of the video had scared her more than she thought. She couldn't explain that. There was no way it was any of her business, of either of their business, really.

'He knows what he's doing.'

She was slipping over a line, into a place where her mother would have the upper hand. She bit down on her lip and turned away.

After a few days in the small room that contained all the evidence of her teenage years Emily wanted to flee. She would have got rid of the lot, but her mother never threw anything out. It did provide some sort of comfort when she visited, at first at least.

She tried to phone Allen on his mobile but, despite what he had said, he had blocked calls while he was out of the country. Can't even talk to my bloody boyfriend, she thought. What sort of a fuck-up is that? Lying back in bed, thinking of him, remembering his body and his strong touch. He pisses me off, she thought, but he's quality.

She'd never met a man quite like him before. None of her previous boyfriends had had such a mystery about them. They'd been flyboys, office workers, one a policeman who talked endlessly about his job but never seemed to have any interest in what she did. Allen internalised the world he worked in. She knew about his past but ignored it. She'd never told her mother, or anyone for that matter, about his bad times. None of their business, she thought.

What she knew was this: he was a brave man but she was the stronger person.

By the end of the week she was missing him terribly. He rang once, sounding lost and a bit scared but assuring her he was fine, things were going well. She missed North London now, it was so quiet here, so empty. What am I doing here, she thought, and, before her mother was up to dissuade her, she climbed into her small teacher's car and drove quickly back to

Islington. The flat, when she reached it, was familiar and wel-coming. Emily placed a few items in the fridge and then phoned around until she'd organised a girls' night out. Let's get hammered, she thought, and forget whatever it is that Allen is driving me crazy with. By eight that same evening she was with her three best friends drinking straight vodkas in a dive bar just off Oxford Street in Central London.

'He's such a dick,' she said, loudly. 'I don't have a clue what he's doing, he wants to save the world, but I'm not sure he even knows what from.' She laughed and her friends laughed with her. Anything that Allen was embroiled in was forgotten for the night.

Belgrade

Late in the night Allen's coach pulled onto the ferry as the passengers slept. Arriving in France at daybreak it set off in an easterly direction, towards the German border and beyond. Allen was happy to be out of London, out of England, on the motorways, looking out over clear, open spaces. For a while this was better than the city. Hours later the coach pulled off the motorway. It was early evening and he had an overnight journey still to come. Time to eat something and stretch my legs, he thought. He climbed down out of the coach and was hit by a blast of hot diesel air. He noticed how clean and tidy this German service station was. Puts ours to shame, he thought.

For a while he lay on his back on the gravel in the thin sun, his coat wrapped around him. Closing his eyes, he felt warmth through his coat, through his sweater and jeans. He sweated and knew that his face was flushed and ruddy in the European heat. He could smell dog shit somewhere near his head in the weedy gravel. He breathed deeply through his nose. The stink was sweet and sour, a thin, ripe odour that came and went with the gentle breeze that whispered around him. It reminded him of the only vacated keepen cell he'd ever visited. The thought made him sit up anxiously. Unsure, he waited for the wind to bring the smell back, unable to conjure it in the intervals. He thought about that dank underground chamber and the normality of disappearance that it had come to represent.

The long-term missing were listed by various agencies on the assumption that they were corpses and it was only a matter of time before a body turned up.

Families and friends would wait years, decades, often lifetimes, sometimes going to their own graves knowing nothing. The search for the lost would eventually peter out with the details locked away in archival boxes stored deep within some vast warehouse, the paperwork now as lost as the person them-selves, stashed away where nobody would ever find them.

All that remained was a wedge of paper in a buff file in a green cabinet in a basement warehouse in the suburb of an un-known city.

Every time Allen read about another missing, he tracked the story and waited for a return or a body. If neither came, he marked the case down and placed a new page on his website. Of course, he had no way of knowing in almost all cases if there was anything, but he was getting the idea. These were not alien abductions. Some of these people were taken by members of our own human race and locked away in confined, dark spaces.

He learned that in any upheaval where a lot of people disap-pear, there are some held against their will. His rule of thumb was, after three years they became keepen – the unknown, who whitened and lost their teeth in damp underground containers across the world.

Online there was something of a conspiracy theory – the sub-ject had garnered its own long tail of obsessives, each with their own theory. The right wing, the left wing, the neocons – they all argued about whether this really occurred, the num-bers, the reasoning and, most controversially, about specific cases where suspects and locations were bandied about. In a way, this network of concerned citizens and kooks came to replicate the much darker network of criminal abductors, sex offenders, paedophiles and the likes, the network that Allen closely monitored and tried to infiltrate for his own research. It was this network, he guessed, that had brought him today's contact. It was like making contact with alien life for the first time. He wasn't going to lose the connection.

The press wasn't interested in the misery of others and tended to the internal explanation: that these missing people were either runaways or had been done to death. It never seemed to occur to them that they might still be alive some-where.

Every few years, somebody would emerge from darkness or a bound situation. Often these people were not known of before the moment of their emergence; thus, they were never listed as missing, even though they had endured years of captivity.

Given no evidence of continuing life, Allen knew that the police would often abandon a search for an abducted or missing person at an early stage. They would keep up the investigation, of course, but as a missing, presumed dead job. Absence of evidence of activity is given as a guide to death. However, locking anyone in a secured cell has the same effect. No credit cards will be used, no phone calls will be made, no passports applied for. No work records, no use of national insurance numbers. The person has effectively disappeared. And death is, indeed, where they have disappeared to, though these deaths are lingering and long-lasting.

If you ever spent twenty years inside, in the darkness, in a basement, you might emerge insane.

He had made the trek across Europe in the past to visit emergers, people who had resurfaced. He wasn't a policeman and he wasn't a detective. But he did have a mission.

He was especially interested in the living dead, abductees who were kept alive deep underground, in chambers and cellars and carved-out cells. Some in luxurious secret apartments and some in dank worm-infested holes in the ground. They seldom emerged, but that didn't mean they weren't out there.

If you have never been incarcerated so deep that you never see daylight, you will not be able to imagine the effect this has on the senses.

Allen knew this, but it didn't make it any easier.

In the distance the coach engine revved and the horn sounded. He jumped up, feeling hungry. Emily had made him egg sandwiches and a scotch egg. She was good at scotch eggs. They were in his bag on the coach.

He stood up, his legs momentarily hobbled by pins and needles. He stretched out his toes in an effort to shake off the ague and looked over to the other side of the car park where a line of huge European coaches sat in the early spring sunshine. He wondered why he hadn't found a cheap flight. Coaches seemed romantic, when in reality they were uncomfortable, hot and smelly, though at least he'd have time to think.

He climbed back into the cold, quiet interior, aware of the fusty aura. The coach was full and Allen looked for the seat he'd been in before, all the way from the 9 am departure. He didn't want a window seat, what passed on the outside now was of no interest to him. The coach growled into life and made a slow circumnavigation of the car park, pulling out onto the anonymous slip road and then down and out onto the anonymous motorway. The sky was flat and grey and the sun fell swiftly towards a flat German horizon.

Swapping drivers every four hours, they sped on towards a second night. Allen talked to the passenger next to him. Deep in the night the man had pulled a thermos of hot coffee from deep in his bag and offered Allen a thimbleful. He'd gratefully accepted it and fallen into a slow, low conversation that took them across three countries. They talked about Serbia and England, the old Yugoslavia and how countries were torn apart, families, children, parents, grandparents, wars, jobs and politicians. This man was a migrant worker, who had fought in the Croatian campaign. Allen shivered at that, but it all seemed a long way in the past now. He stared out of the window as they discussed greasy spoons and plum brandy and the relative merits of football teams, leagues and championships. Lunch was grabbed from a service station on the E70. The Europeans paid for this road, said the anonymous man, as an apology for bombing us. Allen laughed.

On the Sunday morning they entered Serbia. Everybody was woken and tossed off the bus to stand sleepy and shivering in the early morning chill. Stony-faced border guards walked slowly up and down the line, gesturing for passports and holding them open as they compared them to the person standing in front of them. After a while they lost interest and left. The driver found a breakfast stop somewhere outside Zagreb and Allen hurriedly ate a white bread roll and gulped a hot, instant coffee. Then they drove on into the morning, swapping drivers along the way. In the early afternoon, as the sun shone weakly, signs indicated the approach of Belgrade. Clusters of tower blocks dominated the city's skyline. A succession of flyovers, housing projects and industrial areas spread alongside the motorway, towns and villages, as small outliers of the main city eventually became merged into the outskirts of the capital. Slip roads ran away into unknowable areas, mysterious locales that nobody ever visited.

From the open countryside power lines started to run closer together; lorry parks clustered next to shopping arcades; street furniture increased. Allen sat in hypnotised silence as the inexorable growth of the city enveloped them. They were drawn in quickly, surrounded by a network of ramped concrete roads and power substations, canals and traffic lights, more and more, faster and faster as the bus wove through the increasingly dense road system, twisted by camber and centrifuge until the open countryside was gone and they were descending into the core of the city.

On all sides his perspective became limited as clusters of concrete buildings came to dominate his view. The driver, practised in his route, swapped lanes regularly and ducked and dove, now up, now down. The buildings leered at them, now close, now far. Fragments of roads, echoes of schemes planned but never finished, or even seriously embarked upon, drew the eye up side-alleys and into the openings for underground car parks and service roads.

At that time of the morning nothing was quite real. Most of the city still slept as Allen's bus rushed deeper into the cold grey city, stopping occasionally for incomprehensible reasons in unknowable corners to drop off individuals who quickly disappeared into the warren. Allen pondered his belief that you should never get off the bus until you have to. Never exit any situation before you are made to. Exchanging comfort and security for the unknown is a risk that you don't have to take, he thought. That morning as he anticipated the end of his journey his mantra worked in two ways: you had to finish the journey; you had to get off at some point.

Watching the outskirts of Belgrade fly past, Allen realised that under every city is a negative city, a reflection of the endless buildings and tower blocks and shopping malls and stations and roads and canals. Under every tower, a smaller mirror version, dug deep into the ground, entombed, and locked away. An entire megalopolis, he thought, that few knew about – but that few included takers and keepers.

He had once asked a civil engineer how much subterranean space there was under London. More than you can imagine, came the answer, tiny spaces and vast football pitch-sized embrasures; staircases and wells; rooms with no windows and arched Roman vestries. Everything that had been built left a trace, a subterranean space.

There were people who sought out these secretive spaces and attempted to penetrate them for their own gratification, seeing in these liminal spaces a sort of man-made cave system, to be explored and mapped in the same manner as vast water-washed limestone scourings under the Chilterns, entered through an impossible child-sized hole in a city hillside, dangerous for the potential brick fall or onrushing of a forgotten underground stream in flood.

From his vantage point high on the bus, Allen took the opportunity to peer into every window, garden, backyard and private space revealed to him. A woman tumbled out of a doorway in jeans and bra, fell and held herself from collapse for a moment by her fingertips, then caught her balance and turned and shouted into the black cut-out of a doorway. Through a window a couple lay on a bed, entwined in the grey morning light, naked. The man looked up from his position underneath his partner and caught Allen's eye, accusingly. Over there a child emerged, blinking, into the morning light, a school satchel on its back, socks pulled up tight above shining black shoes. A fat man sipped an espresso on the doorstep of a sub-urban bar with a blinking neon beer advertisement, *Flitch Pilsner.*

Then the bus turned onto a wide, tree-lined avenue and he realised they must be close to the centre of the city. Allen pulled his jacket closer around him and anticipated getting up and off into this strange city. They travelled down this thoroughfare for a while and then, suddenly, with a whooshing of brakes, the bus pulled up sharp, pneumatics going whish. Then an impossibly sharp turn took them into a tiny alley where the sides of the bus almost touched up against the grey striated brickwork on either side. Allen, in slight shock, found himself staring for a second into the eyes of an old man, with no hair, in a vest, who stared out from a grimy, almost impenetrable window. Then he was gone. More whish, whish, whish, and the bus backed with a bip, bip, bip into one of dozens of coach parking spaces in a cavernous bus station.

Allen pushed his legs out in front of him before he stood up, stretching them tenderly in the aisle as he waited for the doors to open and the crush to clear. He scanned the view out of the window, looking for a skinny bloke wearing a leather jacket, waiting by the police booth. You can't miss him, the contact had said, because he won't miss you. He'd better not.

The passengers, thrown into intimacy during the long strange night, were suddenly strangers again, looking for their welcoming parties or shuffling off to find buses and taxis or the shared cars of family and friends. As always, he felt isolated, a stranger not only to the town but to the language and to the manner of things, to himself. He tried to imagine what he looked like, standing there, waiting for his luggage. He tried to appear confident but that involved making decisions. He wanted to take his time, to find a coffee and a sandwich, to find a vantage point from which he could survey the city centre. It seemed important to get his bearings before making the next part of his journey.

A hand clapped him on the back.

'Allen?' He turned quickly. A skinny man with bad teeth in a leather jacket smiled at him.

'Hello. You look for me?' He made a steering wheel motion with his hands. 'Allen?' he said.

'That's me,' said Allen.

'Boss sent me. Car near here,' said the driver. He stuck out his hand. 'Stefan,' he announced. Allen shook the offered hand weakly and Stefan motioned to follow him.

He didn't like the centres of towns. It seemed as if every square foot was spoken for or fought over, but he knew that there were always corners and shards that were up for grabs, overlooked and forgotten. On the outskirts, in the suburbs, in the industrial zones there were bigger spaces, basements, nooks and crannies where a sort of life continued unseen. He was interested in this architecture of space, of places where an underclass operated.

They exited the bus station, Allen walking behind Stefan, and crossed a few streets before entering a public square where a large black Mercedes was parked badly, half on the pavement. It was the type of car that East European lowlife drove, Allen thought. Stefan opened the boot and Allen dumped his bag among assorted junk. They climbed in. The floor was littered with cigarette packets and paper junk and it smelled in the musty way of cars that were over used, that were almost lived in smelled.

Allen settled into his seat while Stefan negotiated a complex route through the city.

They drove quickly out from the centre and by way of an inner ring road to a housing estate. Stefan pulled to a sudden halt in front of one of the vast slabs of flats. He gestured upwards. 'Seven floor. Seven,' he said. Allen climbed out and retrieved his bag from the boot. He slammed it shut and banged on it. Stefan leant his head out of the window and shouted 'Party later.' Then he gunned the engine and was gone.

Allen looked up at the block. These were the buildings he'd seen, in the distance, from the motorway. Up close they were hulking monsters from an old school of socialist architecture. Pile 'em high and fill 'em cheap, he thought. He looked across the landscape. There was nothing much else out here except more of the same, circling the city, each block surrounded by identical towers that stretched out across the hillside in serried ranks. There were more blocks beyond these, as if an insane authority had decided to cover the whole landscape in big white buildings with minimal variations between them. These towering structures, the worst but somehow also the best East European architecture, made in the service of a nation where such ideas could be imposed from above. They had crammed their breeding young into these warrens, built when this was still Tito's model socialist paradise. It didn't look much like a paradise.

They stood solid on the landscape, rooted to the rock under the surface. After the war in the great dream of state building, engineers and gangs of displaced people were brought in to create a workers' realm. These labourers weren't slaves, but there was little choice. You worked and you ate. Otherwise, maybe the chance to walk across the border to Greece, to try and reach Germany, but few took that route. They saw the plans, the gleaming modern metropolis, and they worked, they dug and they carried. This was no Chinese-style mass mobilisation. Tito wanted to emulate Stalin, he trained drivers and construction workers by the thousand. Together they excavated deep into the soil, drilled and blew out the bedrock and planted what became Eastern Belgrade deep into the rock. Under the buildings they constructed shelters against the coming onslaught from the West, a place where every citizen could take refuge. There was to be no Swiss solution, the citizens were not to be trusted with guns, just hidey-holes in case the capitalists came for the country in the night.

The hidey-holes were built but locked against intruders. The cadres initially held the keys. But as years passed and these huge spaces were never called on to fulfil their purpose, those keys started to be traded on the black market along with cheese and tobacco and wine. The dark caverns under the feet of the tower dwellers filled up with whatever needed to be kept away from the ever-wider gaze of the police. Things that needed deep, dark containment were taken down and locked away. They were the perfect spaces to get on with your business away from the ever-present watching eyes of the state.

Allen strode into the building through double glass doors to a smell of stale cabbage and alpine rose disinfectant mixed. He looked around for the lifts, but when he got over to them a large sign proclaimed them out of use in language he could not read but which he could well understand. Same all over, he thought, and started towards the stairs, his bag over his shoulder. Concrete step followed concrete step and he started to sweat slightly as he climbed higher, floor by indistinguishable floor. By the time he got to the fifth level he realised there was someone leaning over the banister high above him looking down. He stopped for a moment to get his breath, leaned on the steel banister and craned his head back, looking upwards at the silhouette above, but couldn't make out who it was. Then he slowed his pace for the final two floors while his mind raced to anticipate the meeting. He took a glance up and the face came suddenly into focus. He knew this face. His heart accelerated.

He hadn't anticipated knowing the contact but he realised that it suddenly made a lot of sense. Flushed and sweaty from the climb, he stood and gasped for air. Roger looked down at him with a degree of hauteur.

'Roger?' he said. 'What the fuck!'

'Come in, old chap. Come in. It has been a while.' And as if they were meeting for a drink at his London club, old friends or colleagues, Roger motioned behind him. One of the doors that lined the corridor stood wide open.

Roger

Allen had met him in prison. Roger was doing a stretch for some form of abuse, something involving abduction, Allen was never clear. Roger never talked about it and, if asked, he would wave the crime away with an exasperated flutter of his hand, as if it was all something of a misunderstanding. He was educated and erudite, worth a bit of anyone's time. He hadn't been born into privilege, but a good teacher had spotted potential and pushed him into a grammar school from where he'd scraped into Cambridge. He turned himself into a typical lower-middle-class graduate, the type that rose with effortless ease through the ranks of whatever organisation they first encountered. Roger became a large, solid hunk of an Englishman with floppy blond hair and an inane grin. His chosen profession was in the civil service. Anyway, he had landed on his feet. Eventually he left the civil service and somehow found himself a contract working for his old department as they rolled out some form of support through Eastern Europe. This had become both his opportunity and his undoing.

He had a full beard, short, blond, and dark around the edges. Blond hair gave him the remains of a boyish look, though the rough straw-like quality of it also made him seem more grown up than Allen felt. Allen wore his hair cropped short. Although he often had stubble by the afternoon it always made him feel untidy and grubby.

Roger had a fruity voice. Allen was sure he was putting it on, but it was the sort of pretension that had so grown on him that it had become part of his personality. It fitted with his girth, straining to escape his shirt. He was a type, large but not horribly fat. Dandruff on his shoulders. Very English, uncomfortable in life but comfortable in his large suit. He took out a handkerchief and wiped his brow.

Roger was not a nice man. Not because of the prison or because of anything that had ever been done to him. He was, on the surface, a lovely chap, an old-fashioned type, who would go out of his way to help you out. Back then when they'd shared a cell, Roger had been sweetness and light itself. But there was always the incontrovertible issue of what Roger had been in for, which led to fundamental questions about what went on in Roger's head. And more than what went on in Roger's head, what went on in Roger's life. The nastiness was hidden deep inside him. He had bad interests, as he put it.

Roger led Allen into the flat. The BBC World Service played on the radio, a story about two British men who were handed over to the US military in Afghanistan turning up in Morocco. They had accused the British intelligence services of being complicit in organising their torture. The Foreign Office had issued a statement saying that they never ordered or condoned torture.

'Spent much time in Belgrade before?' Roger said.

'What?' said Allen, realising he was listening too hard to the radio and not really listening. 'Oh, none.'

'Lovely place. Full of thieves and murderers, but great for business. They'll rip you off good and proper if you don't watch them. You have to come down hard, you understand? Hard.' He punched one fist into the palm of the other hand and looked Allen in the eye. Then he laughed.

'Come on,' he said. 'It's not like that here. Actually, it's a bit of a soft town. The Albanian boys have sorted them out. Drink?'

'Whatever,' said Allen.

Roger picked up a bottle and two glasses from the sideboard and gestured towards Allen.

'How are you doing? You seem to have found an interesting career.'

'I'm working on it,' said Allen. 'How about you?'

Roger paced around the room with large strides, past the windows that overlooked other similar blocks, round the sofa and back beside Allen. Then he said, 'I've got this flat. I bought it cheap, they started to privatise everything. It's not the nicest of places as you will have noticed, but it's quiet – I don't get bothered. It's like a home from home. I come out and drink myself stupid sometimes. I've taken to the local brew. Anyway, somewhere along the line I decided I wanted somewhere to stay, and I found this crap-hole. Funny thing is, I really like it.'

He did sound contented. It wasn't as if there was any point in making it up to Allen. Why would he be interested in what Allen thought of his circumstances?

'It's like my holiday home, if you like this sort of holiday. It's my corporate headquarters as well.'

He laughed at this joke, then said, 'I've got a girl here now, too.'

Allen took the proffered whisky and sat down in a fat armchair.

'I'm not really surprised,' he found himself saying. 'I thought you'd land on your feet.'

'Well, it's taken a long time,' said Roger. 'After I got out I went back to London. I thought I could pick up where I left off, but that was all closed off to me. I couldn't even get the time of day from my crowd. I went on the piss for a while, thought I was going to become one of those guys you see on the street. Then one day I got an offer of some work out here, and I never looked back.'

'Have you still got that house in London?' Allen said. 'The Glory House?'

Roger scowled at him. 'Of course,' he said. 'But I can't live there now.'

In their cell together, during their prison time, Roger had told Allen a story of his missing cousin. He said that, when he was seventeen, he had quite incredibly inherited a house that had belonged to a great aunt. She had lived unexpectedly on and on, into her hundreds. Nobody else from her family or friends had lived anything like as long, leaving her beached and alone for decades. It was a large, gloomy house in North London, no use to a seventeen-year-old boy. His mother insisted that he offered it as a home for her recently widowed sister and he did so, grudgingly.

He never forgot the house was his. That was much of what mattered. It gave him heft and ground, it stood him apart from anyone he met and those who came to know him. After university he moved in with his aunt and cousin. Sometime around the end of the last century, when she was a teenager, his cousin had disappeared or, as Roger put it, run away with a man from the motor trade.

After that life had changed in the big house, Roger said. He and his aunt became closer, relying on each other. His life set him apart from his family, who had remained in their small, tidy, middle-class semi-detached and terraced houses. He stopped seeing much of them. After a while he never saw them at all. Roger took his own route through life.

'But what the fuck ...' He stopped suddenly and called out. 'Alicia.'

A small, attractive but worn-down woman emerged from somewhere towards the back of the flat, wiping her hands on her apron as she came. 'Alicia,' he said, 'this is Allen. My friend from England.' She walked forward hesitantly and reached out a hand. He shook it. It was soft and warm and childlike.

'Thanks, love,' said Roger, and the girl disappeared back where she had come from. 'She's cooking,' he said by way of explanation. 'She's always cooking. And she's shy, poor love. Her English isn't very good.'

'How did you meet her?' Allen asked.

Roger leaned in, whisky in hand. He became serious. 'I bought her off the internet,' he said, sober and cruel. 'I bought her lazy arse from a Serbian who thought there was no life left in it.'

Allen shivered; he couldn't help it, the room seemed to go cold.

Roger let out a huge laugh. 'Actually, I found her online. Eu-roPersonals, on the internet. Find your Serbian Soulmate. I thought that was so ridiculous, I had to give it a go. I sort of knew that all the girls were scams one way or another. But I got chatting to this bird, and after a bit she invited me out to visit her. I was getting a hard-on every night about her, so I thought, what the fuck, let's go. She sent me all these pictures of her, all sorts, you know, with her tits out and much more. I'd never met a girl like that before, though I never thought it was really her. But I didn't care too much. Just wanted a shag. Or a bit of fun.'

Allen wasn't convinced.

'You know what? It was her, it actually fucking was her, all the pictures and everything; everything she said turned out to be true. Except, of course, that she didn't have any money and she desperately needed to get married.

'I came out here,' continued Roger. 'Said I'd meet her. Didn't expect much. They were waiting for me, of course, the family. A guy who said he was her brother took me back to his flat, wouldn't let me out again. Nothing nasty, but I was trapped. I'd fallen right into it, hadn't I, right slap-bang into a trap. He kept saying I'd spoiled her honour or something. I had to pay a thousand quid just to spend some time with her. But, you know, it was love, for me; I'd fallen for her, or I thought I had. After a couple of days, I went and got the money out and I really didn't mind. After that, it was all roses, I stayed with her in this little bedsit thing, and she seemed to like me. I hadn't planned on staying long, though, and when I tried to do a runner it turned nasty again, worse this time. Four guys picked me up and took me away in the boot of their car. By the end of that little escapade, I couldn't imagine leaving without her.'

'So, what happened?' said Allen.

'Then I actually did buy her,' Roger said. 'But that was what she wanted. Really, I saved her. They were a gang that had brought her in from Ukraine or somewhere, and I bought out the contract.'

'Somewhere like that? You don't know?' Allen swallowed a laugh, sensing this was not the moment. 'How much does someone like that cost?'

'Over ten grand. Luckily, I had a bit of dosh handy, know what I mean? You just met my ten-grand bride.'

A stupid Rolf Harris song that he'd known as a child was making a repeated circular pattern in Allen's brain, something about kangaroos, then letting his Abo go loose, Bruce. Something he couldn't quite place.

'Anyway,' said Roger, refilling his drink, 'how are you, old chap?' He advanced across the room and took Allen in a bear hug. 'What are you doing these days? It's been so long ...' He tailed off.

'Eight years, I guess. I'm a writer. Well, I write a bit,' said Allen. 'Happy to meet your missus.'

'Well, don't get fancy. She's not my missus. She's a tart. A tart that I look after. My tart. I wanted you to come here to meet a few good fellows,' said Roger. 'That's all I invited you for. We were having one of our meetings and I thought it was time to get to know you a bit better. Can't do any harm, can it? After all, you're almost in the same line of work.'

'Almost,' said Allen and he looked away.

'Tomorrow, everyone will be here. Look, you've got your own room. Alicia even changed the sheets.' He laughed. 'Put your bag in there. I'll make you a cup of tea, then we go out.' Allen would have liked to relax, maybe even sleep for a bit, but Roger had other ideas. He took his bag into the back room where a bed was made up. Next to the bed was a small table with a book and a lamp on it. He lay down on the bed and picked up the book. He looked at the cover. *The Collector.* The woman brought him a cup of tea and placed it on the bedside table. Allen tried to read but his eyes closed quickly. The next thing he knew Roger was standing at the end of the bed.

'Come on, old chap,' he said. 'Time's pressing on.' He jiggled from foot to foot as if he couldn't wait to leave. Allen climbed sleepily from the bed and followed him out of the flat.

They took a taxi down to the commercial sector where expensive Western-style shops jostled for attention with glittering cafes and car salesrooms.

Crossing the road on Priznin Avenue, a car swept at speed past them but struck a small wiry dog that ran out from behind a parked scooter. The car rolled over the dog's hindquarters, rolling and stripping off skin and fur from both legs and leaving a bloody mess. The dog rolled and writhed in the road, yelping and shuddering. Allen and Roger winced visibly and then hurried away from the scene, crossing the road slightly further down. Roger looked visibly shaken. Allen, hating to have seen this, wanted to do something but instead followed Roger further away, down the narrow street.

Roger ducked suddenly into a doorway and Allen followed him. Above the door were the words Lion Club on a tacky plastic awning. A girl sat at reception, she kept her eyes down as Roger and Allen swept through into the reception area beyond. The reception area was decked out in far too much marble and gold with mirrors filling the space in between. Across the back of the room a low couch stretched from one end of the room to the other. The couch was lined with women, none of them wearing very much. The staff obviously knew Roger well and they deferred to him in a friendly, affectionate manner. Allen could smell the room, though he wasn't sure what the smell was. Drains. Or something unwashed. Or fear.

Roger sat down at a table at the back. He pulled out a chair for Allen. A waitress brought two small glasses filled with a clear spirit. Roger said 'Cheers' and drank his in one. Allen lit a cigarette to delay the inevitable. Roger lit one too, though he didn't look like he was interested in smoking it. He laid it in the ashtray.

The women didn't look happy. Their faces smiled at the men who clustered across the room from them, but their eyes were dead.

After a few minutes of talking to the thick set men who stood at the back of the room, Roger got up and walked across to the women, moving slowly down the line. The women preened and disported themselves for him. Eventually he stopped and looked across to Allen. He gestured by moving his head for him to join him.

He knew nothing of brothels and working girls, he had stayed away, maybe for fear of contamination or maybe what he might find out about himself. Better to keep out of temptation's way. He shook his head. He wanted nothing to do with this. He wanted information, insights, knowledge. But not to engage with Roger's prostitutes. He knew it was a test. If he took the bait, he put himself on the same level as every punter who came through the door and lowered himself to the level of the rapist.

Roger, tiring of his refusal to choose, selected a young dark-haired girl for him from the throng and she led Allen through a door at the back of the room. A concierge handed him a towel and they walked in silence down the corridor and up some stairs. They entered a small room containing a narrow bed and a table. The girl pulled back a curtain to reveal a shower. She motioned to Allen to use it. When he emerged, the girl was sitting on the side of the bed. She lay back, pulled off her pantyhose with a deft movement, lifted her knees and opened her legs in a classic pre-coital pose. She made a hurry-up motion. An image of Emily filled his mind, Emily lying in bed smiling at him, Emily getting undressed. Allen turned away and dry heaved. Ignoring the crying of the girl, he dressed quickly and ran back down the corridor, emerging into the reception area with a crash, pursued closely by his assigned hooker. Shouting broke out and the cold-eyed security men emerged swiftly from a side room, bearing down on Allen. Roger quickly held up his hands and smiled at them.

'He is my friend,' he said. They returned to their videos, satisfied that no robbery or assault was in progress.

Roger didn't seem bothered by Allen's refusal to engage. As they left the building he was in a talkative mood. 'Those girls,' he said, 'they'd frighten anyone off sometimes. Anyway, she's not really the point. I'm offering you an opportunity. Call it a partnership, if you want. I'd like to work with you – if you are interested?'

'What can I do?'

'I think you understand us. I can make it easy for you.' Roger glanced back down the road and lit a cigarette. He offered one to Allen.

'Look, the world is filled with basements, with cellars, underground spaces. I have money but, more than that, I have the contacts. But you, Allen, you know more than me. And you were a military man, you are intelligent. I need someone like you. I need information.'

Allen wasn't sure how to reply, but Roger continued. 'I can give you a present, if you want, you know, if you're interested in helping out.'

He did feel a strange attraction to this dark world, incomprehensible to society, to the idea of total control, subterranean lockdown. He wouldn't take the bait, not really. But. For now, for a moment he could see how this could proceed. He'd been on the edge of society before, been places that most people wouldn't even know existed, been locked up for years. He was an army man, he knew the value of discipline, how it worked, how the soul could be broken in the service of the bigger ideal. But this was pushing it. It was an almost religious experience, the lure of takers and keepen and their hollow, hidden shrines, their lost contents.

'I'm not interested,' said Allen. 'It's not for me.'

'But I think it is. Why have you come out here? What do you want, then?'

'I'm a writer, I wanted to understand, to fill in the gaps. You know, I've been chasing you guys, your stories, round and round for years.' Allen shook his head.

'Let me bring you into the club. I've always wanted you to join us.'

'Tell me about the Keepers. I need to understand what you do. It's hard, you do something terrible, as if you hate the world. Do you hate people, or just the people you snatch?'

'It goes back a long way, further than you might think,' Roger said. 'There have always been takers and there have long been keepers. There have always been keepen. At one point it may even have been sanctioned, legal. It's like a parasitical relationship – one parasite, one host – but after a while it becomes difficult to work out which is which. Of course, not everybody wants to be keeper, not everybody can understand the relationship. Not all parasitical relationships are mutual. Do you understand that?'

They stopped in a respectable restaurant – what looked to Allen like a Western pizza chain though he couldn't read the menu – where several of Roger's friends were waiting for them.

'These are my friends,' Roger beamed, pointing around the table in introduction. 'Ekra, Olaf.' Several more names followed. They all looked the same to Allen and he quickly forgot most of their names. They ordered huge pizzas and drank several bottles of red wine. After that they moved on to a bar that was similar in design and modernity: a long, slick walnut and chrome bar, hundreds of some strange local brew stacked up in a lit alcove above the bar. Wall of water toilets, the usual. Here they knocked back a single beer each.

Then they moved on to what Allen would call a traditional European bar. Unlike anything in England, it was still old-fashioned in a modern way. Smokers sat quietly in corners and eyed them as they came in, their group now getting a little rowdy. They spread out across three tables. Ekra delivered a stream of beers from the bar and Allen found himself relaxing into a conversation with Olaf, who told him proudly that he was a master builder. 'I build cage for Marc. For Marc.' He prodded Allen in the chest as if that would help him understand. 'You know, man in Belge take girls lock in cage and they die, take more girls.' Allen realised what he was talking about halfway through the jabbing, a horror story from Belgium. Olaf insisted that they sampled the local spirit, which turned out to be a vodka of dubious quality but copious quantity.

After a quick succession of tiny glasses, Allen ducked out of the smoky atmosphere into the clear air of the street. He flipped open his phone and found Emily's number. She answered almost immediately. 'Hello, love.'

Silence.

'Are you there?'

'Hello, Ems. Sorry, just wanted to say hello.'

'What's wrong?'

She could hear something in his voice. Suddenly he wasn't sure what he was phoning about. Or, he did know but he couldn't say it.

'Just out and about, you know. Anyway, I just wanted to hear your voice.'

Drunken fool, he thought, don't start on the homesickness. He waited.

'What are you doing?' he asked eventually, into the silence.

'I'm sitting in Costa. Having a coffee. And reading the paper.'

'That's good.' Sanity, he thought.

'Allen? Please come home. You don't have to stay. What's the point?'

'The point is, I'm getting something. I think. A good story. I'm close to a story.'

Roger joined him on the pavement outside the club, putting his arm around Allen to take him away from the comfort of London and Emily.

'Better go now, love,' Allen said to her. 'Got to go. Bye.'

He flipped the phone shut and cut her off mid-sentence. Roger raised an eyebrow at him, trying to pick up on the conversation.

'I thought maybe you were sick,' said Roger.

'Just a bit of air.'

'Someone interesting?'

'My partner.' He didn't want to let Roger any closer.

Roger took him by the elbow and marched him down the street, friendly and attentive but in control, suddenly ducking them into a tiny basement bar and ordering brandy for both of them. They drank it fast, Roger making conversation and Allen straining to hear over the loud Baltic turbo-pop that was blasting out, listening, waiting.

'Do you want to take a look around my little empire of dark? Visit some girls? Is that what you're here for?' He changed the subject suddenly. 'Remember when we last met?' Roger's languid approach didn't fool Allen – he knew quite well when they'd met. He must have known the year, the month, even the day. The last day of Roger's stretch, just before dawn. In that stinking cell, talking shit.

'You told me you were going to make your fortune,' said Allen. 'You said you had a plan.' He could recall exactly what Roger had been thinking, but he didn't want to make it easy. 'Something to do with foreign tarts,' he offered.

Roger leant towards Allen. 'When I left jail, I was a bit fucked. My family didn't want to know. Job was long gone. I walked out of that pit with nothing. Now I'm in the import export business and I'm a success,' he said.

'Import export?' said Allen.

'Girls. Bints. Tarts. Buy low, sell high. I buy 'em and sell 'em. I know where to get them cheap, and I know how to sell them high. I know how to trade them, that's where the money is.'

Traded. That meant driving across Europe with a human being stuffed in a van or the boot of a car.

'Traded, how?' he asked.

'In a van. Sometimes in a box. Sometimes rolled up in a fucking carpet. So what?' said Roger. 'I pay for them. That's what counts.'

'You buy them?' said Allen.

''Course they're bought. Not always for cash, though. Sometimes it's to pay debts, or they're swapped for other stuff.'

'What stuff?'

'Come on, Allen,' said Roger. 'You know all this, don't come all innocent with me. I'm not teaching you anything here.'

Swapped. Jeez. This was class.

'You know what,' said Roger. 'Money makes everything alright with most people. Remember what I said back then in the jug? I was going out to make money. Lots of money. So that I could carry on doing what I wanted to do but without the hassle of having the police on my back. That there was always a legal way to do things and an illegal way to do the same things. I'd noticed that prison was full of men whose crime was to be of the wrong sort. Or, to put it better, to be poor and of the wrong class. It always seemed to me that you could get away with anything, like killing someone if you wish, or stealing large amounts of money, if you approached it from an attitude of effortless superiority.' He coughed and reached for his drink.

'Do you know about the relative values of different, shall we say, illegal activities? Most of those guys in prison ended up there not because they chose to become criminals, but because they didn't choose what sort of criminals to become. I realised that they had fallen into their specialism through utter chance. Whether they were any good at it or not didn't seem to matter to them. At some point in their lives they had started out being, say, a robber or a lifter or muscle, and, finding that it worked some of the time, they carried on doing it. More to the point, so long as there were others around them who reinforced their sense that this is what they were good at, they never really thought about what the point of it all was.

'Notice how they were really in love with payday. They, almost to a man, had convinced themselves that they were experts and that this was their chosen way of life. The fact that they got regularly caught and bunged inside for longer and longer stretches never seemed of any consequence.

'I bring girls in from East Europe, all over. They go to the saunas. It's a good business, nothing too heavy. I'm a small player in this game, Allen, but I know the ropes. I have to put money down and then I go to Bucharest or Pristina to see them. I put down the cash, then we arrange delivery. Delivery isn't much of a problem, there are routes, you know. These girls, I own them. They go to work across the country, from here, Belgrade, down to the south coast. It's a busy life, I drive a lot of miles. But I make a lot of money.

'I don't look after them all myself. Well, really I sell them on, but I keep an eye on them.'

'Are they slaves?'

'Most of them I guess you could call working girls. For sure, they aren't really expecting such a hard life, but that's their problem. If they fight too much, they become keepen. Or worse.

'This trade started because there were more girls than we knew what to do with. Now they have more protection and there are fewer. They are less stupid, so we have to work harder. There are laws, they keep introducing laws. It's no fucking good, they can get all the laws they want, it won't stop. Fucking EU.'

He was losing it. Allen wanted the real story, not a paranoid rant. He thought that Roger might have been taking his own drugs. He had never heard such a confession from a trafficker. He was fascinated but didn't know where this would go.

'What do you get from it?' he said.

'Money,' said Roger. 'Money and satisfaction. You know I worked for the government?' he said. 'I was a good boy. I went to my university, even though my father said I never would. I made a new life, I invented myself, got a good job in the service. You can't even imagine how set up I was. Even today, I could walk into many drawing rooms, private dining rooms, where the power happens, and it would be as if nothing has changed. Good old Roger, they would say, he has been away. How are you Roger, how are things?'

'Shit happens,' said Allen. He knew what had happened. Roger had done a stretch as a sex offender. If people didn't care it was because they didn't know the real Roger.

'What happened,' said Roger, 'is that I got tricked and trapped. That, and my own fucking needs.'

He leered over the word needs, pushing Allen to read a life-time of depravity into that single word.

'What happens is that thousands of men, women and chil-dren get brought into this country every year. They come in lorries, in cars, in aeroplanes, in ships. They come because they want to come, and they come although they don't want to come. They come to work and they come to marry, but mostly they come to fuck – even if they don't know that. It's all about money. They come from the poorest countries there are. Don't think they're queuing up from rich places to come in with me – there are other routes for those people. These people come in if they want to or don't want to. Sometimes someone else wants them to come in, they're just the contraband.'

Roger was sweating heavily, it dripped around his collar.

'I provide a service to the shittest of the shit. Don't get me wrong, they are good people. The girls don't argue. Once they are in, they mostly get passed on and I never hear from them again.'

Unless you own them, thought Allen. 'Mostly?'

'Unless I own them,' said Roger.

Allen saw that Roger had created a sacrament around trapped people, that the souls in his caves were there for some almost holy reason. They were sacred places where his followers could worship. But what a bunch of followers, the dross of a post-industrial Europe, fucked-up labourers and professionals with the same calling. They told each other that there was some validity to this behaviour, that a higher calling cancelled out the evil they did. But Roger was adamant that he'd created something new in the world, and something not new.

'It's an old, old practice. It comes from ancient times. You have to understand that. Originally it was voluntary but in time it had to become involuntary, of course.'

The others caught up with them and Roger swiftly stopped talking. After that it ran from good to bad, as it so often had in his past. As the alcohol kicked in, Allen got into a big argument with a tall, muscular man called Carlos, though neither could really understand what the other was saying. It was one of those very drunken arguments where the original point is soon lost.

'Anyway,' he said, 'Roger likes you.'

Allen had moved on from caring, resting his head on his arm on the wet table, but that sentence brought him back into the room.

'What?' he drawled.

'He never invited a real outsider in before. Will he be showing you his keepens?'

Allen grunted, pretending disinterest. 'I didn't know he had any,' he said.

'Oh yes,' Carlos said. 'He's got a whole zoo, under his flat.'

Now Allen's ears were pricked awake. 'Under the flat?' he said.

'Well, you see, downstairs,' said Carlos. Carlos looked nervously across at Roger but he was deep in loud conversation, shouting to be heard above the music. Allen didn't see – couldn't see – how that would work. He knew he was too inebriated to think, but he put the knowledge away for the morning, telling himself he'd better fucking remember.

Then they were up and there was another bar, even smaller, crowded with stony-faced men in leather jackets. Here they drank a strong aniseed spirit in small glasses, throwing them back every few minutes.

'The motherland,' shouted a ruddy-faced drunkard in a leather coat. 'The motherland,' his party responded and they downed their shots. 'And fuck the Jews,' countered the drunkard, but they ignored him.

Allen's grasp on the world, and later his memory, slipped from this point on. They were stumbling down a dark street, he and Roger, holding each other up.

'Whereiswe, wherethefuckiswe,' he slurred over and over until Roger told him to shut up.

At one point he woke up in a doorway that smelled of piss, all alone. He jumped up in fear and staggered out into the road. Catching sight of Roger outside a brightly lit shop , he shouted, 'Fuckyou, what you doing?' at him.

Roger gestured with a wrapped food item. Allen could feel the ocean of alcohol he was swimming in. He felt sick and knew that later this was going to hurt.

He came to on the couch in Roger's flat, covered in a big heavy piece of material. He was wearing underpants, T-shirt and socks. He swung his legs off the couch and stood unsteadily, his bladder pressing upon him with its urgency. He felt his way around the walls and into the short corridor, and a grey light.

At the toilet he stood streaming piss, small, sicky shivers running through him. He steadied himself with an outstretched hand on the wall and he knew that if he pissed for any longer, he would throw up where he stood.

Finally, it was over. He straightened up and turned slowly around. The woman, Alicia, stood there in the hallway, in the dim grey light, colourless and naked, her small breasts and black slash of pubic hair exposed in the early morning light. He stared at her, feeling the huge sadness and unreachable fear welling. Then he turned unsteadily and lurched past her, back onto the couch where sleep quickly took him again.

He woke to find her knelt in front of the couch, her mouth around his dick, working the flaccid flesh. He pushed her away and turned his back.

Blackness. Morning.

Allen woke with the dawn light and the usual hangover, and could not return to the void of sleep. He looked around the flat. His jeans were folded neatly on a chair. He had no idea who had put him to bed. Probably Roger, he thought, more likely that woman, Alicia. In the unfamiliar flat he slowly worked himself upright and shuffled across the room to the kitchen. It was clean and tidy, every surface wiped down. Copious glasses and mugs sat in a cabinet. He was used to waking up in filthy flats filled with a jumble of dirty crockery – this one was a pleasure, if anything with a raging hangover could be described as such. Finding a glass, he filled it with water and drank deep. The water had an unfamiliar tang, something chemical but not too unpleasant. He wanted his co-codamol, his headache pills, something for this ache, but knew he'd forgotten to bring any with him. That was par for the course, never the thing you wanted when you wanted it.

Finding his way back over to the sofa where he'd spent the night, he looked for his watch and found it stuffed under a cushion. He lay back full length and closed his eyes, willing sleep to return. Nausea swept over him again and again, but just as he thought a dash to the toilet was becoming inevitable, he unexpectedly lapsed into sleep.

When he woke again, Roger was sitting in an armchair at the foot of the sofa holding a cup of tea. He nodded down to the floor and said, 'I made one for you.'

Allen's phone rang. He scrabbled around for it in his trouser pocket. Emily. Desperate not to sound hungover, he tried out his voice for the first time that day. She was unhappy with him for not ringing again the previous night. He angled his head away from Roger, speaking low so he couldn't overhear. Not that it really mattered but it bothered him as invasive. Any connection between Roger and Emily, however tenuous, grated on him. He hadn't called, it was true, but there wasn't much he could do about it. He'd been on the piss, she'd slipped his mind, it happened. Had to happen.

'You've had a call,' she said. 'Your mate the copper. Something about a Jennifer. Something new. You should call him. Don't know anything more than that.'

'Thanks,' he said. 'Love you.'

'Everything alright?'

'No problems,' he almost whispered.

'Love you too. Looking forward to seeing you home.' She rang off.

Roger was looking at him a bit too hard. 'Girlfriend again?'

Allen nodded.

'How you feeling, old chap?' he said. 'You do look like shit.'

Allen felt like shit.

He didn't want to be taken in by Roger's posh boy persona – at this point in the morning it really got to him. He wanted to shake him away and lie back down, but didn't feel confident in the other man's house, so he smiled amicably.

'What time is it?' he croaked, reaching down for the hot mug of tea.

'About ten,' said Roger. 'Tea alright?'

'Thanks. Jesus, I felt rough earlier. Feel a bit better now,' Allen said as he levered himself up onto one elbow.

'Well, big day today?' said Roger.

Allen wondered what game they were playing now. He was getting flashbacks from the night before, details revealing themselves to him. Drinking. The bars. Staggering around the backstreets. And then, slowly, a memory of what Carlos had told him: was it made-up boasting or drunken revelation? Under the building? What the fuck did that mean? A basement? Where would the entrance be? He put it out of his mind for now.

And Alicia trying to suck his dick. Fuck, what was that all about?

'What've you got in mind?' he countered. He wanted Roger to reveal his world to him. He wanted to know what Roger had.

The Takers' and Keepers' Club

Roger held Allen's arm in complicity as they left his flat. They walked to the lifts and Roger punched the buttons. After a wait of several minutes, one side opened with a grinding sound and they climbed in. 'Twenty-seven,' he said, leaving Allen to press the key. The lift lurched, wobbled and then moved upwards, slowly screeching and making clanging sounds. No indicator gave away what floor they had reached. After what seemed like several long minutes, the lift crunched to a halt and the door screeched as it opened. Allen looked out. A thin man in a worker's cap stood waiting to enter. A sign behind his head read '18'. The man stepped in, the doors closed unwillingly and the swaying perambulation of motion upwards started again. Finally, the lift stopped again, the doors opened and they stepped out. On the wall opposite a small illuminated box displayed the floor number: 27. Roger turned to the right and Allen followed him out into a similar hallway, the floor covered with mottled grey vinyl tiles, the walls scuffed and marked, painted in institutional yellow and some form of ancient green. The corridor receded into the distance, lit by fluorescent tubes which gave off a reluctant morbid glow. Each side was lined with dark wood doors and on each door a metal number and a small letterbox. Some doors were personalised with a doormat. Very little marked out the different doors. From somewhere came a strong smell of ... what? Antiseptic mixed with cooking vegetables? Roger strode down the centre of the passage and stopped in front of a door with a small square of obscured and reinforced glass.

'Here we are. Righty-o.' He rapped on the door with his knuckles.

Allen felt a wave of paranoia sweep over him. Roger, recognising this, said, 'Don't panic, old chap. They won't be interested in you, except as a friend.' He purred over the word friend. 'You are safe with me.'

Someone pulled the door open, gave them a once over, and they were in. The small, thin man who had opened the door to them and Roger engaged in a complicated routine of hugs and backslapping.

The flat was the same size as Roger's but in reverse, a mirror image of where he had spent the night. It overlooked the motorway and now he could see the distant city centre. It seemed at once both grubby and grandiose, the style of over-optimistic socialist building projects. The room was thick with cigarette smoke: Allen's eyes smarted. A smell of cooking pervaded the flat. Not cabbage, not unpleasant, but redolent of continuous cooking in a small space along with body odour and something else that he couldn't quite place, maybe cough medicine. Sheets of torn material mostly covered the windows and where light did penetrate it fell at an odd angle, picking out patterns in dust and smoke. In the corner the blank screen of a huge, ancient television reflected the scene back to its inhabitants. Underfoot, a surprisingly clean and bright yellow carpet stretched from wall to wall. From a side room came the sound of laughter as a door opened and Alicia emerged, carrying a tray laden with bottles of beer. A group of pale unshaven men slouched on cheap couches and chairs, chatting and smoking. Their eyes darted towards Roger and Allen as they entered, then returned to their conversations. The surfaces of several tables were covered with beer bottles and overflowing ashtrays. It looked as if a party had been in progress for several days and some of the occupants of the room showed signs of exhaustion.

He stared at the assembled cast. Some stared back. This must be them, thought Allen. The faceless ones. Some lay as if asleep, legs spread wide, heads on the edges of sofas or chairs. Some wore American sporting gear, baseball and truckers' caps, chinos. A couple were dressed in military fatigues, others wore tatty suits. Their ages ranged from what looked like a tall, spotty teenager to a couple of old men with sunken eyes who sat bold upright at the back of the room. Some were over-weight, some thin to excess.

As his eyes adjusted to the half-gloom of the room Allen re-alised that there was more activity going on than he had thought. A couple of more smartly dressed men sat at a small table to the right of the room, and a skinny woman passed through with a tray of small teacups. Pushed from behind by Roger, he shuffled around everyone and eventually reached the back of the room.

A tall, dapper man in a dark green suit and tie entered and stood in front of the assorted audience. A buzz of anticipation arose quickly. The bodies took note and sat up to look towards the front. The man looked around with interest, but his eyes met no-one's. He held himself as if he were addressing an au-dience of several hundred, though there were fewer than twenty people present. It was as if he were operating on a dif-ferent plane, not really in the room. He spoke calmly and authoritatively; he was living the subject matter even as he spoke.

He glanced at Allen. 'You all know why we're here,' he said. Allen hadn't expected a formal meeting with a chairman call-ing them to order. He wondered about a rule book and privately laughed at the thought.

'It's good to see you all again. As you know, this meeting is not taking place.' He paused for the small laughs that broke out. He spoke in good English but with a strong accent that didn't seem like anything Allen had heard before.

They didn't know he'd waited years for this moment, that he'd long known of their group but never thought he'd sit in with them. They seemed individually familiar, a cross-section of the underclass of Europe with a few highflyers scattered in. A few years in prison, you meet them all, he thought. They are of a type, there's not much originality in lowlife. Then again, he realised he wasn't much of an original either, if it came to that. Allen's world was filled with people on a mission that they had little chance of successfully undertaking. Not that it mattered now. Here he was, in the lion's den. These are the worst of the worst, he thought.

'Gentlemen,' the man continued, like an affable compere at a pub quiz, 'welcome to the club. I'd just like to cover the ground rules quickly. First, this meeting isn't taking place, of course but, if you get asked about it, we're a carp fishing club.' The assembled room laughed, this seemed to be an old joke.

'Now, I'd just like to explain a few things for the benefit of our newer people.'

'The act of taking has a huge and traumatic effect on the person who is taken, but an even greater psychological impact on the taker. The moment of taking may have been worked towards for months or years, run again and again as a movie in the mind of the taker. Up to this point it is a fantasy. But now it is real, you are in the process of becoming a taker. The act of taking is, by necessity, brief yet intense, violent and overwhelming. To some, this moment is so overwhelming that you do not, cannot, progress to keeping. To the taker, this moment may manifest itself as a still and silent moment experienced as a dream sequence, or it may become a bloody, screaming, inchoate life-and-death struggle. The taken may realise in an instant that they have one chance and that fighting is a high value response, or they may acquiesce in the take, frozen through fear or a lack of understanding.'

He paused and stared intensely at the audience, catching an eye here or there. They sat in silence, maybe dreaming their own dreams or anticipating returning to their lairs.

'Your aim is to minimise public attention from this point on, to effect a clean take and to move on swiftly to the keeping stage. Of course, often the taking is a failure, in which case it ceases to be a take and becomes a news story. It may also, depending on circumstance, become the end of the road for the taker. It may lead to arrest, exposure, imprisonment, disgrace. But, although the success of a take is of the highest order to the taker, without a keep, it becomes just another sad story and is soon forgotten. Pretty much everything will be known about it, about you, shortly, even if you make no mistakes. The taken may be released, freed or killed. Whatever the outcome, a taking without a keeping is a failure and does not bring you within the ambit of the Takers' and Keepers' Club.'

'Now,' he announced, motioning to the front row, 'I'd like to introduce you to our host. You all know him well, I'm sure. For those of you who don't, I'd like to introduce the man who has made all this possible: Roger.'

Roger made his way quickly to the front of the room and smoothed down his jacket. He spoke slowly but confidently, as if he were the founder of a charitable organisation that was recruiting new supporters. His English was immaculate with the clipped cadences of the South.

He explained how the Keepers grew out of East European prisons in the seventies through contacts made and knowledge of crimes committed. He was, he says, by no means the founder. The real founders could not be here today. The room laughed knowingly. The group was well established, he went on, when he came across it, but it was a loose, inefficient network of like-minded individuals rather than anything effective. It was, he says, his idea to turn it into a well-structured support organisation. Here, several of the men in the room sniggered into their hands but Roger ploughed on without pausing.

He described vaguely how members were identified and recruited. He waved into the fog of the room.

'Please welcome David,' he said, 'and Mikey. And, um, Sid.' The lanky teenager grinned from the back of the room and gave a circular wave. 'That's me,' he said with a grin. Roger mentioned a few more names and then continued.

'We are well organised now. Our network stretches across Europe and deep into the old Soviet sphere. There are now swaps across Europe, people are taken in one country and spirited into a different country for "keeping". This works well,' he laughs, 'for police forces generally can't handle the idea that a missing person is not only not dead but is in a different country.'

He gestured at two tall, thin men standing at the back of the room, both wearing spectacles and what Allen thought looked very much like dog collars.

'Rashim and Leden, our theological brothers.' He waved to them and they waved back, smiling.

'They are very good at what they do. It's based on the tradition of solitaries, of anchorites. You've heard of them? People who shut themselves away from the world, often by being walled up in small rooms attached to the church.'

Again, Allen felt a sickly chill in his gut.

Roger explained that although many takers are amateurs who abduct for sexual or homicidal ends, once they decide to become a keeper, they encounter many more complex issues. Often the keeping ends very quickly and violently, or with the arrest or death of the taker. He said that many of the techniques of the takers come from the human traffickers 'out of the East'. While it is possible to buy a victim to hold on to, and that these prizes are generally untraceable, it is not a common practice. At this point Roger grinned at Allen, then at Alicia, who was still handing round drinks.

Roger continued, pointing out that while there were always people around who would never be missed, that wasn't necessarily the point. 'So, someone is not missed, so what. Better to take someone who will be missed, very missed. Do you understand my logic? If you do your work properly, after a few days everyone will think they are dead. They will eventually be forgotten about, even if you have provoked a huge police hunt. Then you get the pleasure of knowing, year after year, that that is not so.' He smiled thinly as if imagining something that only he knew. 'You have heard of Fred West,' he said. 'He and his wife, they took girls, runaways, in their own town. They even took their own daughters. No-one missed them. He wasn't a keeper though. He was just a thick thug. He might have wanted to keep them, but he never prepared the ground – and nobody really knew who was gone. Fred and his wife, they weren't keepers. They could have been but they were fucking ordinary takers. Murderers, really. And we're not murderers. Always remember that.'

He finished and returned to his seat. A lanky boy stood up and talked about the internet and how he had built a private network where the security is so tight that the police could never break it.

Allen whispered to Roger: 'You make it seem so ordinary. Like we can all have a girl in the cellar. There must be police out looking for them. How does this happen? If I grabbed some bird off the street in London, all hell would break loose.'

'We're just mutual support, help in times of difficulty, if things go wrong. They don't generally, though. Remember, many takes are never reported. They are not even snatches, they are the result of careful planning, wives acquired for that purpose, daughters even. The police tend to look in the wrong direction because they think they are dead, or they don't even know they exist.'

'How many in Europe?' Allen asked.

Roger said he guessed that there could be as many as a hundred, possibly even more if the former Soviet Union was taken into consideration.

'Read the papers, take a look into the archives. How many of those disappeared people do you think are still being held?'

'I know the archives,' said Allen. 'I know the numbers.'

A man that Allen recognised, the man who had picked him up from the bus station that morning, sidled up to them and looked like he wanted to join the conversation.

'Ah, greetings, Stefan,' Roger said. He looked at Allen. 'You've met, of course. Stefan was in the war, you know. It fucked him up, things went from bad to worse, but he came out alright in the end. Didn't you, old chap?' Stefan grunted.

'War?' said Allen.

'He fought through the Bosnian campaign, the stories he tells, they'll scare the skin off you. He brought back a keepen, though, so it wasn't all pointless.'

Allen said, 'War booty?'

Stefan didn't smile. 'It is rendition,' he said. 'My right. When the Americans kidnap terrorists and hand them to countries who don't give a shit. They can torture information out of them, without it being illegal. I play the same game.'

'Allen was in the army,' said Roger. 'He probably knows all about that sort of stuff. Don't you?'

Allen grinned. 'I was a lowly squaddie,' he said.

Roger suggested quietly that they should talk. He steered Allen across the room, between the low tables, and motioned to Stefan to follow. He pushed Allen towards a doorway and into a bedroom. It contained a dishevelled bed, a small table and a couple of chairs. Allen sat on the bed, Stefan and Roger took the seats.

'Stefan is an expert,' said Roger. 'He's like the military wing of the Takers and Keepers.'

Allen looked at Stefan. He didn't feel comfortable in this company but he had to let them take him in. 'You're the big cheese, then?' he said. 'You know where the bodies are, um, buried?'

Stefan looked confused. 'Roger is the boss, Mr Allen. He created this and we look up to him. He is the boss of the takers. He's an honourable man, to us. He protects us.'

'Protects you? How does he do that?'

'He knows the police, the authorities. He has money and he uses it to keep them away from us. I don't know.' He tailed off. 'He just makes things happen.'

'You understand,' said Allen. 'that I'm interested in meeting some of your keepen?'

Allen looked quickly at Roger and then back at Stefan.

'Tell him about yourself,' said Roger.

Stefan had a look approaching contempt on his face, but he started anyway. 'First, I was in Bosnia, in the war, all over.

Special forces from the Bosniak towns, we were the hardest of the hard. We learned to live in cellars, we kept our enemies in cellars and when they left the cellars, we killed them. There they had no fucking choice because we sat and waited for them to emerge. I killed women with a spade, it was the work for the Serbian fatherland. Either they fucked me or I cut their necks with my spade. I got a taste for it. I lived in cellars. I only came out to fight, to fuck and to shit. My officers, they hated everyone, me also. After the war, no work, no money. I went to Germany and I met a man called Ekra and he brought me to this.

'Now the Americans want to take me to Holland, to the court, for what happened in the war. I can hide anywhere around Europe. Sometimes I put myself in my underground bunker and wait. But I have my own prisoners, they are secure and they will never escape.'

'You make it seem so fucking ordinary. Like we can all have a girl in the cellar. There must be police out looking for them. How does this happen.'

Roger smiled at him as if that was the most stupid question he'd ever heard.

After the meeting had ended and they had got back to the flat, Roger announced that he had to 'go away' overnight. He didn't tell Allen where he was going. 'I'm taking Alicia,' he said. 'Don't worry about a thing. Make yourself at home and when we get back we'll go and visit some of my girls.'

He showed him the kitchen, where the cups and the coffee were. He pointed to a pie in the fridge. 'There's some gibanica for you. The Serbs love it, you must try it.' He smiled at Allen. 'Enjoy. Drink the beers too.' He handed Allen a key and then he and Alicia were gone.

After they left Allen peeked out through a tear in the window blind in the sitting room and watched them cross the parking lot and disappear towards a small business park, Roger holding

105

onto his wife's hand as if he was scared she might disappear. He scanned the horizon, trying to orientate himself. There were parks, a fair bit of greenery. Another cluster of housing blocks loomed.

He felt strange in their flat alone, the combination of trust and abandonment unsettled him. He was at their mercy, what was he supposed to make of that? When would they be back? It was as if this was a test, that they were offering him a challenge – or a trap. He wondered whether the police had any interest in this strange group. He knew that in London they would be watched and infiltrated already, but maybe out here nobody gave a shit. It was a strange place. He knew he should take the flat apart, to see what might turn up, but he couldn't make himself. No doubt the place was clean. After a while he ate some of the pie and drank a beer from the fridge and settled down for a long evening on his own with only Serbian television for company.

Stefan

Something was wrong, but he couldn't put it together. He was in a car, on the backseat, and when he tried to lift his head, it seemed to be stuck to the headrest. Morning sunlight strobed into his eyes. Nausea rose in him. It was as if he was drunk, but he knew he hadn't been drinking. He tried to focus on the person in the front seat.

'Stefan?' His voice wouldn't quite work properly. There was no answer. 'Where are we going?' He couldn't remember leaving the flat. He couldn't work out what had happened.

'Stay calm,' said the voice from the front. 'You wanted to see this. Now you get a chance. But it is dangerous, you have to trust me. It is for your own protection, there are dangerous people who would like to know what you know.'

He remembered Stefan promising him a trip to his caves, then realised he had been drugged. His head felt heavy as a sack of potatoes and he let it drop back to the cold vinyl. He remembered many hungover missions with friends where they would drive and he would lie prostrate on the back seat, moaning, hands over his head, trying to keep the nausea down. He slid down, out of the light, and it felt better to be horizontal, wedged between the back doors.

He drifted and woke. They were still driving. There were lorries, horns. They stopped, started, in some sort of traffic jam. They seemed to be passing the same place, or he was going crazy. His eyes wouldn't work, he couldn't recall. Then he passed out.

He came to with his head enveloped in a thick black sack. He sweated into the darkness, almost panicking, before reminding himself to breathe slowly through his nose, a survival technique he had learned in the army.

Stefan called out, 'You alright, Allen?'

Then nothing.

When he woke again, Allen found he was lying on a low bench in a small room. As the anger and fear passed, he pulled himself up and stood against the wall, then walked carefully out, into a corridor lined with doors, each with a small reinforced glass window. He paced to the end, past doors with ribbons and photographs pinned to them. The photos showed young women, looking into the cameras. Some as if in love for the first time, or serious, having their high school or passport photo taken, others fearful, browbeaten, livid, broken. Some faces were made-up as schoolgirls, others plain, staring. Some doors had more than one photo pinned to them, and fragments of older, removed images.

He banged on the nearest door. Then on the next. He pulled at the handles, but they were locked. He lifted a small hatch in the first door and peered through, then jumped a good yard backwards. From inside the cell a human locked eyes with him. He held the gaze for a few moments, the brown eyes in a pale face looking into his, unwavering.

'Hello,' he ventured.

'Yassa.'

'Who are you?' he asked, but the ghostly figure shrugged back at him with a deep, lost despair. He lifted the flap of the next door and peered in, but there was no occupant. Every other cell was empty.

He leant against the wall for a while and considered his situation, then, with an urge to find a way out, he started moving faster, peering into a room with a low bed and a thin mattress, and metal rings set into the floor. At the other side of the room stood a worn purple couch with pink cushions. Magazines were scattered on the floor and two plates, seeming to contain the remains of a meal, sat on a round rug. The contrast chilled Allen. Some sort of waiting room, he thought.

The lights went out.

On a timer, he thought. Some remnant of light remained, a sort of glowing limelight. He couldn't work out where it came from, but it gave everything a dim iridescence. Through a long horizontal slot he could see a light in another space, connected to this one, but at a different level, higher up or lower down. There were more spaces. How many, and how deep did they go, he wondered?

In the dim light he felt like the first man on the moon in a black and white movie where he had to move slowly, or in a diving bell at the bottom of the sea with no air. He slowly lifted one leg, then the other, and stepped sideways, trying to remember the layout of the dungeon. He turned around and could make out the doorway through which he'd entered this room. Far away a woman cried softly, not sobbing but a mumbling moan of someone unhappy and frightened. Or maybe a warning, he didn't know. Slowly he made his way back to the room where he'd started and lay down.

There must be more people here, in the cells, he was sure, on different levels, behind other doors, wretches captured and held. It was Roger's domain, his world of keepen. He shouted, but there was no response. He swivelled his head around and stared into the gloom, but the harder he tried the less he could make out. He blinked, again and again, waiting for his eyes to adjust. After a while he convinced himself he could see the edges of the space in the stygian deep – here a doorway, an opening, a corridor. And there, a human figure.

He blinked. Nothing. Now he was imagining things. 'Hello?' he shouted. A very slight scrabbling sound in the dark, then again, nothing. I'm losing it, he thought.

After this, during a period when he wasn't sure if he was dreaming or not, a tall woman with long matted hair came and stood over him, watching him sleep. Each time he opened his eyes she was there and he closed them again immediately. This wasn't something he could handle.

He was dreaming between the dream, if it was a dream. He was in cars, on the top of buildings, with no brakes. He wanted to drive down, but instead rolled slowly to the edge of the roof where he found the brakes didn't work. And then he woke and didn't know if he was still in a dream. But the white lady was standing over him in the dark, looking at him with a fearful expression.

He wondered if he still had the hood over his head, but how could he see this woman if he had a hood on? She seemed real enough – when he reached out his hand she recoiled back into the dark. He woke again, and she was squatted in the dark against the wall.

His world filled with endless dreams of ghost-like women who stood over him, sometimes holding cups of water to his mouth. He didn't know whether these were figments of his imagination or inhabitants of this dungeon, but even in his dreams he knew he was trapped, that Roger had tricked him and somehow Stefan had kidnapped him. He knew he was close to ending up a keepen himself.

And this repeated and repeated and finally there was nothing.

Eventually he woke fully and everything was different. The light was on and hurting his eyes. He twisted to look up, his body aching all over. Stefan stood there, his blue suit crumpled and dusty. He was holding a gun, pointing it at Allen. He looked down at him with a wry, pitying face. 'So, you see how it is, my friend. Have you seen enough? Do you like his children?'

It was some sort of a game, but what game were they playing?

'Help me,' Allen said. 'I'm hurting.'

Stefan crouched on his haunches and stared into Allen's eyes. 'You feel good now? Think you still rescue girls from here?'

It wasn't a question.

'How you like to spend a few years in this? You like that. Nobody knows where you are, gone from the world. You are in the depths, down with the underworld.' He laughed.

Allen looked around the space. He seemed to be in the corridor of some military bunker. The walls were studded with metal bolts.

'This isn't right. You don't need to lock me in here.' A memory of army training came to him. He was desperate now, his mind searching for an escape.

'Don't matter,' said Stefan. 'You stay here, learn to live with it. The girls live here ok, so you can too.'

A chill ran through him. He didn't want to spend another minute here. He could feel the effects of drugs wearing off, leaving him nauseous and shivery in the damp gloom of the cellar.

'What girls have you got here?' he asked, wanting to keep Stefan talking, to keep him there, close. He knew that if he left, turned out the light, locked the door, it could be a long time before he had another visitor, another chance.

'You are a spy and a fucking idiot,' shouted Stefan. 'A cunt sent to betray us,' he grunted, demonstrating his education in the English underworld.

'Come, now. You will stay with us for a while. Roger wants you. You are value. You are property now.' He spat out the word property to give it its true meaning. He waved the gun, motioning towards the corridor and took hold of Allen with his other hand, dragging him along the floor. Allen levered himself to his feet and skidded along, heel after heel, in an attempt to remain upright. He slid along the rough concrete floor until Stefan pushed him into a dark cell and slammed the door shut.

In the dark Allen could hear the faint whine of a fan spinning, somewhere in the depths, and feel the slight movement of stale air around him. He wondered how deep they were, how many locked doors there may be between him and the surface. Despair started to creep into his bones. So deep, so deep. This must be a military-civilian bunker, he guessed. Yugoslavia had been

111

riddled with them, built for the elite to survive war, whether war came from the West or the East.

Tito had been paranoid, not without reason. He had spent forty years building hideaways deep under his cities, but after his death many of them had fallen into disuse. Since the end of the cold war there had been little interest in these sepulchral chambers that riddled the Serbian earth. While some had been converted for storage or even nightclubs, many others were left to rot, their doors chained shut and abandoned to the earth. They weren't hard to come by, if you knew where to look and who to ask. Many city buildings had them, as did hospitals, police stations and government buildings. In a broken Serbia, few questions were asked if you took a hammer and a chisel and re-opened a cellar of your own.

After a long wait someone made a sound outside the door. 'Get me the fuck out of here,' Allen shouted as it was unlocked. A torch shone on his face. He scrunched his eyes, trying to see who it was. Roger's stare fixed on him, but gone now was his wide smile. He looked at Allen through half-closed eyes.

'You're a clever fuck, you sure are. Poking, probing. I thought we were friends.'

'For god's sake, Roger,' said Allen, 'I'm a writer. I'm not trying to damage you – we're friends, or something. I'm not coming after you.'

This is it, he thought. This is how I end up. The mystery is solved. I become one of them, an underground dweller. Suddenly it seemed all too real.

Roger stared down at him. 'With your nose in my business, I have the right to protect myself as I want. You may not understand this, Allen. You are fucking with fire here.'

Allen tried to jump up but Roger moved quickly and clamped his foot down hard on an ankle. Allen swallowed a scream, then relaxed. He waited to hear what Roger wanted. He realised he had come close to something that really mattered to him, the existence of these subterranean human hostages.

Roger stared at Allen for the longest time. Then he started to speak. 'I'm having difficulty making sense of you. My friends in London don't trust you. I heard from my contacts that you are a danger to me. Are you? What is your game, Allen? Are you working with the police, trying to trap me, to turn me in? Why are you so interested in my keepens? Do you think they exist?'

Allen wondered whether the shapeless forms who shared this space could hear the conversation, whether they were listening and waiting for the outcome.

'If they exist, it's because of you,' Roger went on. 'You want them to exist. You wanted to find your keepens. I've got a business to run, I don't need your help or your fucking input. I've got my own family to look after. Keepens, keepens, fucking keepens.'

Roger's voice climbed the register. 'Every problem comes from your meddling and everybody we lose is down to you. You have to learn just to stay away from the subject. It's nothing to do with you. You're a little pisser playing up big and it has to stop.'

Then he stamped down again on Allen's ankle. This time Allen screamed loudly. Bastard, he thought.

'Roger, it's not like that,' Allen said. 'We're two sides of the same coin. I know nothing about your business, it's not you I'm interested in.'

'You're not interested. So not interested that you crossed Europe and put yourself in a hole to avoid me. I know what you think, our girls are worth shit. But we look after them, feed them, clothe them, get them into the country. That's what they want. But sometimes they won't keep their side of the bargain. Sometimes we sell them on. Sometimes we have to use force. But sometimes we lock them up for a while. It's our police force.' He laughed. 'Stefan has learned from me. He's also my policeman, and very good at it he is too. These girls don't get missed. They come from all over, who knows where they've gone to? They are runaways and whores. We buy and sell them, cheap as chips. It's been going on forever. It's not anything new. Even the police can't keep tabs on it. There are too many, and we move them fast. If one or two go missing, who's to notice? They'll never be missed. And even if they are, what's to be done? By that time, we've got them deep in a hole, deep under the ground. It's always been like that, through history. How many girls do you think have disappeared under the ground and lived out their lives in darkness? And did anyone care? How many have been rescued?'

He paused.

'Does that turn you on? Would you like to fuck a keepen? A twenty-year keepen? Can you imagine how they become, what their flesh is like, how it is to be in the presence of someone who hasn't been outside the walls for decades?'

Now Allen felt sick. He knew many cases, he had the notes, of men and women who just disappeared from the face of the earth, always presumed dead. Abducted. Murdered. But not locked up underground. But it was true, it did happen. He had known about it for years, the lost souls of Europe. It happened, but there was something about Roger, something he had long wanted to work out. He played the role of organiser.

'Tell me about it then, Roger. What do you do? Is that your thing, locking them up underground? Rape? Control? Hate, or love? What's it about?'

Roger looked thoughtful for a moment.

'You'd never understand it. You're not interested in the power; you just want to spoil things. Think about this: if you lock someone up for a week, they are angry. After a month they are unhappy. But after a year, they are yours. They don't think they'll ever get out. Ever.'

Allen looked straight into his eyes. 'Tell me, Roger. How long? How long can this go on for? Even you won't be around for ever.'

Roger didn't answer. He turned around abruptly and walked to the end of the corridor, reached up and swiftly climbed a ladder attached to the wall and disappeared through the hatch at the top.

They listened for a while to the sound of Roger climbing up and out of the depths. As the sound receded into the distance Stephan turned to Allen with a wave of the pistol. 'Get in the cell,' he said. Realising this was his last chance, Allen summoned his long past army training and, in a rage of fear and loathing, snatched at Stefan's gun which whipped from his fingers and spun away into the darkness. Stefan roared and lunged at Allen. They fell to the floor and struggled for a what seemed like hours, battering against each other until, with a shriek, Stefan fell back, splayed out on the concrete. Allen rolled away. He held his breath, watching for any movement but Stefan stayed motionless on the cold floor.

Allen looked around, judging the entrance and exit of this hole. He wasn't in the mood to play horror movies. Upstairs there was light and the world. He wanted to get back up there and reintegrate himself.

He pulled open the green metal trapdoor that Roger had exited through and swung himself through the gap. He found himself in an antechamber. Pulling open the door of that chamber, he saw the bottom of a concrete staircase. He rapidly climbed the staircase, two stairs at a time, up and up. Repeating this again and again, he counted the levels, five, before he reached a top where a grimy doorway blocked his progress. Around the edges of the door he could feel air – this was an exit, meaning he was at street level.

He banged on the door. Then he tried to find something to pull on. He could not get it opened. Then, finding strength, he pulled with full bodyweight at the cross-member of the door. The door flew open towards him and he flew backwards and down the the stairs, painfully. When he picked himself up, he saw a rectangle of good, honest sunshine and a view of the nearby buildings. He felt in heaven. As he suspected, he'd been deep underground, below a stack of normal flats. He looked up and realised he had emerged from underneath Roger's building.

He ran through the lobby and into the stairwell. He feared an ambush by Roger or even that Stefan would free himself quickly and emerge from the cellar. He climbed swiftly, now the third, the fifth. Soon he was back up to the seventh floor. He stood gasping in the open corridor outside Roger's flat. Then he hammered on the door, desperate to find his passport, to leave. I can handle this, he thought. I'll smash his fucking teeth in. No answer. He hammered again, shouting and banging. The flat was silent.

Pulling off one shoe he smashed it through the window to the right of the door, reached through and opened the window which folded back and down upon itself. He pulled himself up and through the broken frame, then fell, heaving and out of breath, onto the floor of the kitchenette. He was frightened, very frightened. His heart raced.

He turned and looked slowly around the flat, seeing how empty it was, had always been. No pictures on the walls, no books, no possessions. He ran into the bedroom where a huge double bed dominated, covered in a powder blue counterpane with a vast bolster. He pulled open bedside drawers. They were empty.

The flat already felt abandoned. He rifled the space, searching for evidence of occupation, but there was none. He had been fooled – nobody lived here, this was a dead flat. It now looked like a squatted property, used and jettisoned.

He ran through to the back room and into the box room where he had spent the previous nights. His possessions were scattered across the floor. Looking into his bag, he saw his passport and his wallet were gone – shit, that would cause problems. All he wanted now was to get home fast and leave Roger and Stefan and the rest of them far behind. He picked up everything he could reach and pressed it into the bag.

Pulling open the door, he ran out into the corridor, down the stairs three at a time and away into the cool evening air towards the distant motorway.

Capture

Emily floated out from a very bad dream to find she was lying on a hard floor feeling cold and uncomfortable with a dry retching in her throat. It was very dark. When she tried to move her shoulder seared with pain. She lay still and then, after a bit, pushed her legs out into the blackness. Where the fuck am I? she wondered.

Staring into the darkness, she could only make out fuzzy patterns. She strained her eyes although she knew that this whorling motion came from somewhere inside her head. I've had this dream before, she told herself, I can wake out of it if I focus. She tried to shake it away and waited for consciousness to arrive. The darkness remained, the hard floor, the cold. She swallowed back the fear that was rising in her chest. She tried not to think about where she was.

Her arm was twisted under her body. As she gently extracted it the blood began to pump back through it and to her shoulder, which now hurt even though she didn't move. Stinging pain spread from her right shoulder and back, as if she'd been dragged along the ground. She could feel the cold everywhere, right deep down into her bones. Her upper body ached and the muscles in her hips hurt. Her left leg throbbed as if something had grated down it. When she flexed it, she could feel abrasions all over. There was no feeling in her feet, it was as if they had gone.

Where the fuck am I?

No matter how hard she stared into it, the dark would not clear. The space became more oppressive, it started closing in on her. Now she could hear the size of the space. It stretched far away from where she lay. At least I'm not in a coffin she thought, not in a car boot. Not in a wardrobe.

Is this the game – to guess where I've ended up?

Maybe I've had a stroke, been run down, crushed by a lorry. I'm lying in a hospital bed, locked in with no sight. Soon a doctor will come to my bedside and talk soothingly to me and my recovery will begin.

She moved her hand to her pocket, but her phone was no longer there.

Maybe I'm dead, she thought.

She slipped back into sleep and woke again and again. Things changed slowly. There was no time or space for more than one thought each time she surfaced but she realised that each line of thought represented one waking period. With each period she climbed further out of the mire.

Eventually she flexed her body, trying to move without making a sound. Her mind would not focus, she felt drunk.

One more push and I'll wake myself up, she thought.

A feeling of panicky nausea swept through her.

Blinking repeatedly against the darkness, she tried to hold onto her sanity. I must keep the panic down, she thought, knowing that she would eventually work out what had happened.

She always did.

And then she saw it. A face. A pale, very white girl's face, close to hers, examining her minutely. A small grey face, wide-open eyes, huge pupils, thin red hair, a flicker of a smile playing across the tiny mouth.

Help, oh fuck, make it go away her mind said while out of her mouth in the darkness came a small wailing sound which, before she knew or controlled what was happening, broadened and grew into a huge caterwauling wail, an encompassing cry of fear and terror in the sooty night.

The girl retreated into the dark and, with the soft click of a door somewhere, was gone.

She subsided into sobbing tears.

When she woke for the third or fourth time she was lying on a low mattress. There was a blanket over her. She shivered slightly but the previous chill had gone. Her head felt empty.

She lay rigid under the fleece, trying not to move. Her bladder cried out for relief, but she had no desire to move in case that face reappeared. Earlier she had been lying in the middle of a space and now she was lying next to a brick wall. With a blanket over her.

She pressed her heel against the wall, testing the solidity of her surroundings.

Yes, she thought. It's a wall, properly built. The sort of wall that holds doors in place, that holds locks and beams and concrete and all the things that a human body can't break through. She shivered again.

On that first day she pissed in the corner, staggered around in the darkness and tried to supress the darkest fears that beset her. The girl had disappeared, into the darkness. Emily had no desire to go looking for her.

She found that the floor was cool, maybe glazed tiles, and that she was wearing no shoes or socks. It crossed her mind that she might have been raped, she couldn't be sure, but she'd clearly been beaten and thrown around. Her hips and her knees, her elbows and one side of her head were deeply grazed. She felt the blood coagulated in her hair. She struggled to remember how she might have got here. She had a memory of leaving a pub, of walking unsteadily in a dark street, but nothing more came to her. Her wrists were sore where she'd clearly been bound. She was wearing the same clothes as when she left home.

She tried to work out where the fuck she was but found herself bursting into tears when she thought about it.

There's another person here, she told herself. She thought she'd been locked in hell but she didn't believe in hell – something else terrible was happening. She understood it had something to do with Allen, with his stupid obsession. She briefly wondered where he was, whether he was safe, then a terrible thought crossed her mind: maybe he knew what was happening. Maybe this was part of a project, of his game. The thought chilled her, even though she knew it couldn't be true.

The hours passed slowly in the darkness, her mind raced, chasing after phantoms and awful thoughts. 'Allen, Allen, Allen,' she wept to herself. And then, 'Mummy'.

After a while, she wished the white-faced girl would come back. Anything would be better than this darkness. She sat, arms pulled tight around her knees, back to the wall, falling in and out of sleep.

The first days were terrible, she knew she could fall into madness – she wondered if she already was. She saw faces in the darkness, looking at her, small faces with wild red hair. She couldn't work out what they were, who they were. There was a woman here, the white-faced woman, and there were children. The faces kept retreating into the dark corners and through dark doors when she moved. It seemed that they were as scared of her as she was of them. They were locked in a cellar with her, she understood that, but she told herself that this could not be real, that it could not be happening to her.

After endless sleeping and waking in the darkness, she realised that it was no dream that she could surface from. The teacher in her came out, she understood that she had to organise the horror so she could understand it, survive it. I have to make contact, she thought. To survive, I have to make friends with them. If they are scared of me, then they are people like me. If they are people like me, I can talk to them. She concentrated on the darkness, watching, studying their movements. When she saw the woman, Emily took a deep breath and summoned reserves of courage, forcing herself not to scream out. She held out her hands in the dark space. 'Come and talk to me,' she said gently. 'Don't be scared, I want to be your friend.'

Then from the stillness came a small voice.

'Over here.'

She swivelled her head, staring intently into the darkness. A mass of bees seemed to buzz in front of her eyes, turning anything that might be there into a fuzzy grey mass. I'm going crazy, she thought, I can't see anything.

'Where is here? What the fuck is this place?'

She felt strange, swearing at the darkness, but desperation overcame her reserve.

Then out of the grey fuzziness the person appeared. A small, framed woman in a baggy dress. This time Emily kept her nerve, not flinching. She supressed the desire to scream.

'What the fuck are you?'

The woman stared at her for a long time then turned again into the darkness. She seemed to move effortlessly through the murk. After a while she returned and handed Emily a cup, touching it against her hand. It was filled with cold water and Emily gulped at the cool liquid. It had a calming effect and her heart slowed to a reasonable rate.

'Where are we?' she asked.

'Don't know,' said the girl.

'How did I get here?'

'He brought you in yesterday.'

'Who is He?'

'Man,' the woman said. 'The man.'

She took a breath, calming a thousand fears.

'Who are you?'.

'I'm Abigail.'

'How long have you been here?' she asked, but the woman said nothing and moved slowly back out of sight. Then, out of the darkness, her small voice said, 'Always.'

Somewhere in the darkness, as Emily fell back to sleep, a baby started to cry.

Home

It took Allen a week of hitching and hiking to get home from Belgrade. He slept in ditches and had a very difficult conversation at the UK border before he could get into the country. He anticipated an angry girlfriend: his lack of contact would not look good. He steeled himself for an argument in which he would again fail to tell her just what had gone on, how strange his trip had been, how close to disaster he had come.

In the flat Emily's things were scattered in her usual manner. A pile of schoolbooks sat on the kitchen table. Her toothbrush sat in the glass, nothing out of place, nothing unexpected, but she wasn't there.

The police arrived an hour after he got there. Two very young constables and Peter Herman. DI Herman was a happy man. 'We're investigating the disappearance of your girlfriend. Her mother reported her gone days ago.'

Missing. The word entered him like a bullet and suddenly the worst seemed possible. Fuck, fuck, fuck, suddenly he felt cold and sick. The air disappeared from his lungs and a strange sound, a wheezing, grating gasp, emanated from deep inside him. His legs softened and buckled. He reached out to hold on to Herman's shoulder.

Herman disdainfully flipped the hand away and said. 'We haven't got much to go on, she might have done a runner or you might have done her in, we don't know at this point. But we'd like to know when you last saw her and what you've been doing this last week.' He took out a notebook. 'That's another thing we'd like to ask you about,' he said. 'We know you arrived at Dover without a passport. Where have you been?'

He could tell them about his trip, but where would it get him, would they even believe him? If she had been taken, and if Roger had anything to do with it, the problem was here in London, on his territory. He needed to sort it out, and fast.

'What about the day you left?' Herman asked. Allen knew the reasoning, but there was nothing. A suspect who had been out of the country – even the police had to acknowledge that it was unlikely – unless a body emerged. That could do for him.

'I've been away,' Allen protested. 'Research, out of the country. I'm a journalist. I don't know anything?' He realised immediately how awful that sounded.

Eventually they arrested him for entering the country illegally and took him, handcuffed, to Finsbury nick. They put him in a holding cell. It wasn't a hardship. He had been in prison before, much harder prisons than this, and for much longer periods. He understood how to survive within a small space enfolded deep within a building. He often thought this was what gave him an insight into, and sympathy with, the people he wrote about.

'Been up to your old games again?' Herman said when he first came to interview him. Allen knew exactly what he meant and how it was intended to be a threat, but he ignored it. His time incarcerated was the result of a fairly predictable set of circumstances. His early life had been one of drift and had ended badly. None of it was a secret, but he didn't spread it around. He had left school at sixteen and drifted around the world, taking badly paid jobs in order to continue his partying in whatever city he found himself. In Australia he'd almost become a serious player in the drugs market before a close shave with the police frightened him into leaving the county. In a moment of madness after returning to the UK he had joined the army and a short, unhappy, period followed. Aldershot, Germany, Northern Ireland, Cyprus, wherever they wanted him to go.

In the army he had a sideline as a dealer, supplying drugs off-base to the locals, an outshoot of his previous life. He wasn't much of a dealer, just a party boy who liked to make some spare change on the side. It was more of a habit, all of his friends had been doing it, buying and selling, whatever drugs swept through. It was a way of life while he sorted himself out, how to get out of the army, what to do next.

Then he sold some pills to a contact who sold some on to two schoolgirls looking for a party night out. They both died during the night. They were just children, fifteen-year-old kids who'd never done much of anything wrong before.

It couldn't have gone more wrong, and for the first time in his life he'd seen how destructive high-profile exposure could be. The tabloids took up a hue and cry against him, calling for an exemplary sentence and then demanding, in a week of madness, the return of the death penalty. A killer of children they called him. The babes in the wood, poisoned by scum.

The press had made it into a big story, man kills girls, like he was some sort of perverted murderer, and by the time they were done with him he'd ended up with a four-year sentence, and it seemed almost unbearably generous. He accepted it, kept his head down and did his time. Self-loathing sent him into a spin of depression. The army threw him out and he spent most of the sentence in solitary, for his own protection they said, though he felt it was more punishment. In the end it wasn't that hard. He spent a lot of time in the library, reading about the world, did some learning, repented publicly. They let him out after two years, on parole. He couldn't travel. Get a crap job, they said, so he did. Then he'd met Emily.

Interrogation. Herman had obviously made up his mind about events even before the first interview.

'You're pretty famous, aren't you?' he started. 'Mr Kimbo, I'm suggesting that you know more about where your girlfriend has gone to than you want to let on. Overdose, was it? You been playing around with the hard stuff again?'

Allen kept his mouth shut. The lawyer that Jenkins had sent over objected, and Herman moved back to a more reasonable line of questioning: when had he last seen Emily, where had he been, what had he been up to?

Even before the end of that first interview, Allen had decided to tell them about Roger. He was fairly sure Roger was involved. He needed to get out, to do his own detective work. Wherever Emily was, she might not be coming out for a long time unless he could … what? He could hardly bear to think about it, so he offered to help the police. 'I've got contacts,' he said. 'If you let me out, I can help you.'

He told them some of what he knew. The police did know of Roger, but they thought of him as a smuggler who worked with East European gangs. He'd never figured greatly on their intelligence reports. Herman wasn't interested that Allen was brandishing his name.

'He's a people smuggler,' Allen said. 'He's been doing it for years.'

Herman looked bored. 'If you think boosting up your old cell mate is going to get you a free pass, you're going to have to give me a bit more than that.'

Allen told them how he'd met Roger when they shared a cell and while they weren't really friends, he had kept vaguely in touch. Roger had become, in the years after the opening up of Eastern Europe, an acknowledged expert in government circles on these networks, the sources of supply, the methods and origins and the destinations of these hapless individuals. He had quickly understood the hooks that this trafficking had in the governments and police forces in the East, but also how they would corrupt institutions in the affluent West. Germany, Austria, Italy and then France, Britain and the northern Scandinavian countries fell for the available charms of his imports. He had developed an interest in the abundant supply of young women from the depths of the newly capitalist countries around the rim of Russia. These women were discovering, to their horror and their country's shame, that there was a huge demand in rich Western nations for their services, sexual and otherwise. And that there were plenty of hard men who would stop at almost nothing to supply this demand. In a few short years, the value of this industry rose to match and then briefly supersede that of international drugs networks.

'Roger rose to the top of that business,' he told Herman. 'He was smart and well connected and developed new methods and new sources of supply.'

It was a brutal business, he said. He thought Roger had fallen foul of other mafia figures who wanted to enter the game, and of his own desires. In short, Roger had preferred the keeping of trafficked girls to passing them on. He was an aficionado of the underground chamber.

Herman said he didn't really understand why Allen was telling him this. 'What's this Roger character got to do with your bird?' he said.

Allen told him about Serbia, a part of what he knew about the Takers and Keepers. He didn't name them and he didn't give details – he was worried it sounded too fantastical. He told Herman a version of what had happened to him, trying to convince him of a bigger picture, of someone else with an interest in taking Emily. But Herman didn't want to take the bait.

'But why Emily, Allen?' he said, repeatedly. 'Why would this bloke snatch you and then your girlfriend? It sounds like a load of bollocks to me.'

Allen didn't really know either. 'Revenge? Ransom?' What he did understand was that Roger's world existed separately from the cops-and-robbers world of policemen like this one. Eventually Herman seemed to realise Allen probably had nothing to do with Emily's fate and released him. The press hadn't got wind of the story. Allen knew that when they did it would be a shitstorm. He imagined Herman was probably holding the story in reserve, knowing how quickly his life could be ruined.

He went to see Emily's mother who screamed at him, told him to get out of her life, accusing him of murdering her daughter. There was nothing he could say in return, he almost felt that he had.

After that he got his head down and tried to push the memories out of his head, but he couldn't forget what he'd seen, where he'd been. And where was Emily? He didn't want to forget about it but he couldn't bear to think about it. He didn't have a solution. He almost wished he hadn't come back, that it was he who was imprisoned in the dark. Somewhere. Down there. An image of a woman in an underground cell, staring blankly into the light as she danced, haunted him.

He went back to his old haunts, to his circuit of junkies and sickos, looking for clues, looking for Roger, but there was nothing.

He probed his contacts in the local force but they'd gone quiet on him, no longer happy to feed him inside information. The heavy hand of a potentially political case had made itself felt. He knew there were coppers who would talk – but they were being kept well away from him. I can help, he told them, I know this world, but he couldn't provoke any interest.

He walked through the back streets of London, a long, endless, convoluted journey, again and again, making a visual check of every doorway, every boarded building and potential opening in the fabric of the city.

On the surface London looked crap in this weather, wet rubbish strewn around the streets, but underneath he imagined it pristine, clean, abandoned but tidy. Why did every city have to be like this, a sump full of people, all concentrating on their own needs, discarding what they no longer wanted, dumping it for someone else to clear up? He knew she was out there, under there, down there, somewhere. The long history of the place had left thousands of forgotten and abandoned spaces under his feet: labyrinths, cellars, tunnels, passages, subways, shafts, burrows, holes, mines, vaults, cantinas, crypts and undercrofts.

The answer was obvious but he avoided it. The people to go to were the Takers and Keepers. HOW? But they now seemed far out of his reach and out of his league.

At home he sat, lethargic, in his work chair. There was no work. He checked his emails out of habit and re-read many from the past, looking for a clue. There was no hint of Emily, nothing, the earth had swallowed her up, literally. When he thought about it, he felt sick, but he had to think about it.

He knew they were watching him; he knew they were digging. Maybe they'd surface Roger before he did. A week passed and Herman got back in touch, slightly contrite now.

'We're going to do a public appeal, you know: you get up in front of the cameras and make an appeal for information. You get to be on TV. You talk directly to whoever is holding her and ask them to release her. Lay it on thick. There's probably a slot on Crimewatch in it. The press is interested and they'd like to have you up there so they can check you out. The press will lap it up. You don't have to show any emotion.' Allen understood the game. If he wasn't a suspect, he was seen as a potential connection. It was a test, but he had nothing to hide and nothing to lose.

They made the appeal, but it turned up nothing. It was as if she had fallen into a void, into the blackest of black holes from which no light could escape.

Jenni

As the weeks lengthened into months, he became consumed by Emily. He wanted desperately to catch a glimpse of her, hear her again, to talk to her and, most of all, to extract her from Roger's grasp. He didn't want Roger to have her. He could smell her around the house, her clothes in their drawers, her makeup and her books, her toothbrush, her hairbrush, containing traces of herself. And he realised how he loved her, how he'd come to enjoy life when she was around. He fell into a deep despair.

Then, after one of his periodical visits to *London Strife*, he stopped for a coffee outside a cafe in Soho to enjoy the sunshine. The medication he was on made the world hazy, but he had started to come to terms with events. As his doctor said, he had to go on living.

A woman walked past, stopped, blocking the sunshine, looking down at him. He ignored her for as long as he could, studiously avoiding her gaze. When he realised she wasn't going to move he flicked his eyes up.

It was Jennifer.

In the summer sunshine she was a different person—older, thinner, well dressed, smiling. Her hair looked as if someone who knew what they were doing had had a pop at it. She was more grown up, almost sophisticated, he thought, if he hadn't known what she was really like.

'Mr Allen! Oh. My. God. It's me, Jenni. Remember?'

The whole world had moved on, he thought, except for me. He nodded.

'Jennifer. Of course,' he said. 'How are you?'

She let out a little shriek, wanting a better response.

He forced a smile. 'You look good. How nice to see you.'

He half-heartedly motioned for her to sit down next to him. He didn't really relish her company, not the half-mad girl-woman he had briefly known, but there was something about her now, something confident and alert. She pulled out a chair and sat next to him, a little too close.

'I saw you on the telly. And in *The Sun*. How cool is that?' She had, of course, but for the worst reasons.

She licked her lips and smiled at him again. Any sense of worth still seemed to revolve around the media.

'Didn't I see you in something?' he said.

He knew exactly what she'd been doing: bit part appearances, daytime chat shows, newspaper exposes, commentary ghost-written for her. There was talk of her own show, *The Survivor* or something. He didn't think it possible that anyone would do that. Exploit her in that way. But who could tell? These days, anything went.

'Oh, Allen, things are brilliant. I've been on the telly. I've met so many famous people. My life has changed. And I'm going to do a book. I've got an agent now.'

He felt a small stab of jealousy. That should have been his book.

'That's really nice, Jen. You're almost a star, I guess.'

They chatted about celebrities she had met and the people she was working with. In the middle of it all she suddenly said, 'Oh, I'm so sorry about your girlfriend, what am I like, going on like this and you must be so unhappy.'

'Yes.'

He didn't want to discuss Emily with her.

'Got any ideas what happened?'

'No.'

She stared at him as if trying to make up her mind. Then, without waiting for a response, she said:

'I still see him.'

'Who?'

'Promise not to tell? The Prick, of course. I see him sometimes. Is that terrible? He won't really let me go, see, it's our project. All this, the telly and all that. It was his idea. I told you. It was our plan. And then …'

Allen waited.

'… I might be able to help you,' she said.

'What?'

'Find her. You know.'

'Jen, don't say that.'

'But, the Prick, he knows things, people. Stuff. He might.'

This is insane, he thought, but he was now alight, burning with desire for more. Maybe she could.

'I'd like … I mean, if you …' He tailed off, not knowing where it went.

'It's ok,' she said. 'You don't have to say anything. I know how to do this. For you. You were nice to me.'

She placed her hand over his. Jesus, he thought, this is terrible. He pulled his hand out and, reaching in his pocket for a pen, scribbled his mobile number on the till receipt.

'Just give me a call if anything comes up.' He stood up quickly. 'Bye Jen.'

He strode off fast, down the road. As he moved away his eyes filled with tears and, when he thought he was far enough away, he balled his hands into fists and croaked out under his breath bastards, bastards, bastards, bastards.

He renewed his search for Roger and pulled out ten years of research, endless notes over newspaper clippings, looking for a pattern. He considered going back to Belgrade, but in his heart he knew there was no way of finding out where Emily had gone until somebody wanted him to know.

Jenkins got in touch, he wanted more stories. *London Strife* was going through one of its periodical cash flow crises, and he needed drama. 'You could do something on that Spanish story. Can you tie that in to London?'

A recent headline had caught their attention: after a year missing a child had been found in the early morning, wandering in the port region of the northern Spanish city of Santander. The boy had disappeared while at a supermarket with his family. The police had made investigations and had quickly decided that the stepfather was complicit. He had been arrested and was still in prison, his trial due, but now the child had emerged, white and shaken but seeming in good health. As with most of these cases, a blaze of publicity accompanied the initial revelation, with photographs and commentary from local judiciary and police. Allen was amazed at how the press in Europe seemed to be allowed, even encouraged, to press in on lost and damaged children, taking photos and asking them questions.

It reminded him of the outcome of the Detroux case a few years previously. The Belgian paedophile had kidnapped two girls and locked them in a secret cellar annex, from which they were released during a police raid. Rather than extract the young girls in a private fashion, the police had brought the scantily dressed children out in the full glare of television and press lights, ensuring a further humiliation was heaped upon them. It was akin to abuse, he thought, like the creation of pornography by the free press. The images circulated after these raids were certainly collected and pored over by the sort of men that Allen cultivated for their contacts and their knowledge.

'Fuck that,' Allen responded. 'I want to write about London. I think we need to make the case that this is a trafficking centre, that girls and young boys are brought here as part of the underground railroad, and then distributed.' He wasn't sure if this was even true, but there were things he wanted to say.

Jenkins held out the offer of a proper job, but he had to write what was asked of him. Even Santander. 'Maybe I can even find you a publisher,' he said. 'Get a book going again.' He wanted to help, but Allen had heard it all before. He didn't want to fall into that trap again.

In July two boys larking around on a demolition site hammered at a metal door they came across until it sprang open. Entering it, they found a succession of small rooms built from scrap metal. When a woman with long hair and fingernails emerged from one of the rooms they fled in terror to the police.

Allen called Herman and begged him for further information but found a wall of indifference.

'Nothing to do with your missus, mate,' he said. 'This is ours, keep away from it.'

Several times he had visited the sites of recovered people, the cellars, basements and underground spaces where crude prisons had been fashioned. Sometimes at the invitation of good contacts in the police, more usually months afterwards on his own initiative, he had clambered down into deadened spaces, pulled out false doors, propped up weighted traps and cages in order to clamber into the human pens that others had ingeniously created. Those spaces haunted his dreams, even when he wasn't dreaming his feet traced the outlines of forgotten cells. He had once been in a small space where two children had died when the air system, for what it was worth, had failed. The space had been thoroughly disinfected, yet to Allen's senses it carried the imprint of desperate and dying innocents. He wondered why children took to imprisonment better than adults. After interviewing some escapees, he knew this to be the case. And still.

He kept writing. He had to, to earn a living, and it kept him closer to the world where Emily was. So he rustled things up without enthusiasm and then was ashamed of them, although he knew eventually something might bring a lead, a word. He realised it was a far more complex world he was dealing with, that it overlapped with his world out here. It was only a matter of time, though that time might be years.

He knew someone still cared about Jennifer.

And he knew someone had Emily.

Down There

This is a life.
The first week was blanked out.
The first month a nightmare.
The first year an existence.
The next eighteen years, an ordinary lifetime.

Around the base of the wall she had scratched a record of one vertical scrape for every time, every fifth visit getting a horizontal stripe across the preceding four. She'd seen this once in a film about the Count of Monte Cristo. She knew it worked, but she never counted the total. It was just for the record, for her record.

Over time you could forget nearly everything. You forgot the things you knew, and you then forgot what you had known, coming to exist in a self-created world where your only references were what was around you and what occurred regularly.

At the same time, you learned a lot of new things. Abigail thought she'd grown up fast, she was rather proud of her grown-up self. She looked forward to a day when she saw her parents again – they would be proud of her, she felt.

Abigail could remember her family, she thought. Some days she could remember them clearly, other days she started to doubt that she'd ever known such a wonderful world. Those were the days in which the cold seeped deep into her bones, the smell of mould became overwhelming and the lights went off inside and outside of her.

Then there were the days that he came to visit.

Remembering rain.

The clock

Routine

Soup

Eventually the child returned from the darkness holding a shimmering ovoid, a hard-boiled egg in its shell, out on the palm of her hand.

'A present for you,' she said in a strange sing-song tone.

Emily shivered back against the wall, as if she could fall through it to get away from this person.

'Eat,' the person said.

'Get away from me.' She slapped the egg out of the child's hand and, jumping from the bed, ran into the darkness, colliding with the wall, face first. She sat down in a heap, blood running from her nose, and cried slowly, for an hour or so. Then, driven by hunger and fear and desperation, she looked round and crawled in the dark to where the egg had rolled. She reached for it, stretching out her arm and picking it up with fingertips.

It seemed strange to peel and eat an egg in those surroundings and she was aware that her hands were filthy, but she took the egg carefully and cracked it on the side of the bed. After cramming it in to her mouth, almost whole, she felt calmer. Looking around, she noticed that the elder child, the one who had brought the egg, was still watching her in the distance.

'Thank you,' she said. 'Thank you so much.'

The child spectre looked at her for a while and then smiled.

'Modher sent it.'

For several long days Emily lay in the darkness thinking about Allen, about her mother, of the sunshine, the world outside. Sometimes she thought 'Fuck you, Allen, this is all your fault, you and your fucking abductions', and she wanted to scream out in the darkness. But sometimes she remembered him with fondness and wanted him to come and rescue her. On these days she felt calmer, though she knew it was ridiculous.

The vapid children would appear out of the gloom and sit on their haunches, watching her and waiting for her to make a move. They now brought her food – bread, tinned fruit, eggs.

She grew used to the ritual in the half-light, the way these young people understood this space and were at peace with it, whereas she struggled every moment to restrain her urge to panic, to cry and shout and run into the corners. Whoever their mother was, she remained hidden away somewhere at the back, in a room to which Emily was not invited.

Her eyes adjusted to the stygian depths and her ears also started to tune in to activity within this realm. She started to understand how it operated – there was a family living in some rooms in the depths, they had access to food and water, they cooked in there. A toilet was plumbed in, there must be outside world reasonably close and a feed of water into this place. But for all her explorations and her pondering on what and how, she came no closer to a solution to her obsession – a return to where there was light.

She made friends with these gentle, strange girls who came and went from the softly clicking door at the back of the space. They showed her around the pitch-dark space, how to find the toilet, where a dripping tap gave water. They brought her food every day from their own secret space and extra blankets for her bed and as the days passed, she became more relaxed in the darkness. She felt her way around, noting where the space grew colder and where it was warm, trying to work out the size and scope of the rooms, where she was and what might lie beyond. If she asked the children where this place was or anything about how they came to be here they said, 'You mus ask that of modher.'

'So where is mother?' she replied, and smiled, but they only gestured with their heads into the gloom.

'Take me to her,' said Emily.

When her children came and told her, there's a lady here, they said, she is nice, they said, she needed some time to think about that. This whole life she had been alone, for so many years she'd lived here with no-one, then her children. So how can you explain eighteen years in a dark cellar? And how do you explain two children, two children that weren't there when you were taken in. How can you explain falling in love with the man who kidnapped you from your childhood and who locked you in the dark for your whole life, who made you his wife by force? Who raped you over and over until you came to accept his love, until you came to enjoy sex with him because you knew nothing else? How could you explain two children born into the damp hole, who have known nothing in their lives but dark and decay. At least you knew light, the sky and the countryside before your life changed to this. At least in a previous incarnation you had walked on grass and swam in water. Down here your children had known nothing but concrete and the packages of food that were brought by their father, your lover, your jailer, their captor. What sense did that make? That whoever you had once been no longer existed, that this life was the only life, everything in the world existed down here, that there was nothing else. That your life now is black and white like an old-fashioned film and if old life was in colour you no longer could think of that. How could you make a start at explaining that to this woman who you didn't know and who you didn't trust.

Every time he came and did that thing she made a tiny doll baby from scraps of wool and cardboard torn up and put it in the back room. No-one else was allowed in that room. A funny peculiar, not funny ha ha thing about him was that he let me make rules and he obeyed them.

But there were some things there were no rules about, but we understood the rules.

You have to accept that I am my own person. You might not think much of me, living in a hole, but I am a family person. This is my family.

You might ask how I know that I live underground. Well, first he has told me many times where I live. He has also told me why I live here, and that I will never be freed.

There are things that I will not reveal. These things are my things. As you can imagine no doubt, it has been necessary to create a story of my life that works for me on a daily basis – to speak nothing of my children. I wanted them to be proud of me.

There are things that I will not reveal to you. There are things that even he does not know. These are my things.

Dear mummy, sorry I didn't come home yet. I crid a lot and missed you so much and daddy too and midgy and smudge. a man took me and he has hidden me in a cellar and I cant get out yet. but I will come out soon and come to find you. if you know where I am please come and find be becasue it is horrible here and dark adn I dont like the dark and the bed is on the floor. plese kiss midgy and smudge for me and I will come home when he lets me free xxxxx abby

Allen

Above ground, Allen couldn't settle or find any interest in what he was doing. Emily was vanished, had been vanished, and the worst of it was that he could imagine where she had gone. When he slept, or when he woke, or in idle moments when he let his mind drift, an image of a spectral woman dancing in a dark cellar came into his mind.

He moved out of his flat, to a rented house, then on to a different flat further away from their home and after that, a few weeks later, on to another smaller, cheaper flat. Throwing off the comforts of home added distance between him and his previous life. He walked the streets keeping an eye close to the walls and entrances, sometimes walking through the night, eyeing up half-hidden doorways and bricked-up windows that hinted at voids within.

He continued his research, though the fire went out of it. Always keeping half an eye out for Roger, he wondered around London and dug into his contacts and networks, but it wasn't a task he could stick to for long. Everyone who might be useful had gone to ground. There was fear going down and nobody wanted to talk to him anymore. They burrowed away from sight and, like their victims, wouldn't be surfacing anytime soon.

It dawned on him that he didn't really know who Roger was. He had to start again from scratch, assembling an image, a picture of him. The stories, clues and evidence mounted, scrap by scrap. He pulled all his research down from his shelves and spent a week combing through it, looking for patterns. Every abduction, every trafficker, every court case. He scanned them all. Each time someone went missing he was there, watching the police search and either find a body or give up as the story slowly drifted out of range. He tracked missing people across Europe, trying to work out a pattern from what was a mishmash of data. Drunks, runaways, domestics, children, mentally ill, crooks, thieves, blaggers, cults, religions, armed forces, work – all these things had the capacity to take people away from their homes in the blink of an eye. So many ways to disappear. Most high-profile cases had nothing in common except for the desperate sadness and anxiety of the families left behind.

But every few months there was something that didn't fall easily into one of these groupings. A disappearance with no explanation, no traces. Then Allen could easily imagine a cellar, an abandoned water tank, a hidden railway arch, now containing a frightened, lonely human locked against the light of day.

Every time he crossed London, and he crossed it a lot, his eyes flickered from doorway to staircase. Every basement entrance, every heavyset door attracted his attention for a moment, but he knew this was no way to find her. He developed a fear of the underground with its myriad tunnels and passages. He knew there were occupied spaces deeper in the system and he feared them.

He kept his ear to the ground. He understood that she might one day be surfaced, if whoever was holding her decided that something was needed, that cover had to be broken. But all his contacts were silent, as if there was conspiracy to reveal nothing. He thought of Elizabeth Fritzl spending twenty-four years underground with her children and how she had only surfaced when her father became convinced her daughter was dying and Allen shuddered. A quarter of a century. At night he wept quietly.

Emily

'You have to understand who he is,' she said. 'He is my father and my husband and the father of my children. We've been together for a long time. I wouldn't say he's the best man I could have asked for, but I've come to accept him. He is all I've got and all I've had for a long, long time. And my children know and love him. That's what a father is, surely?

'I decided to go along with whatever he wanted. Sex, obviously. He was calm but forceful. If I tried to stop him, he would punch me to the ground, split my lip, my nose, my eye. Rape me, then leave me bleeding anyway.

'After time I wanted to make him look after me. If he wasn't going to let me go, I wanted him to suffer for me as much as I was suffering for him.

'If that meant getting him to fall in love with me, you could say that was my plan.

'He never brought johnnies, to stop the babies. I asked him for them. What do you think will happen, I said? He knew, of course. At first, I thought it would bring it to an end, but after a while I realised it was part of the mission. He wanted the babies and that came later. He didn't care, wanted it to happen. Feed the power.

'After the first years I got used to him. The life became normal.

'I think I've been ill. I'm not sure who I am or where I came from. My name is Abigail or Abby or maybe Gail. I've been living in a cellar under the ground for years. Since I was younger, I was twelve. There's a man there, he is my husband, it's official. He told me, we were married by a priest, so everything became alright. I've got his children, they are many years old, they are not babies any more. My husband, he is the father of my children. I never did sex with anyone else before that, so he must be the father. I don't like him much, but I guess I love him.

'He took me from my parents in a previous life. He told me they didn't want me, that they had arranged this. I never believed him at first. As I said, I've been ill for a long time, longer than I can remember. I take medicine for my illness, every morning. He brings it for me.

'He has looked after me, fed me, clothed me. He has been nice to me, I don't want him hurt. My home is under the ground. If you could please let me have some of my medicine?

'Where are my children, please can you bring them to me? They will be scared of you, they don't know about people or the world. They have lived with me in my rooms all their lives, please be gentle with them.

'Take a look at my teeth, what's left of them.'

Message

By the end of July, the days had heated up and made the city an even more unpleasant place. It was one of those seemingly endless humid London summers. Allen twisted and turned in the London miasma, waiting for a clue, something to start the process.

The sunshine was unexpected and after the first few welcome days when everyone put on shorts and sandals and took to drinking beer outside pubs, tempers started to loosen. The nights were as hot as the days. Allen left his windows open but the heat and the blackness outside gave rise to nightmares in which he was searching endless tunnels for Emily and finding only side doors that led into small rooms with gridded openings that dropped further down into blackness. Each time he got down on his hands and knees and peered into the void and caught a glimpse of somebody walking out of sight. He thought it was Emily, but when he stood up in the dream he couldn't work out if it was her or not.

These dreams frustrated him and he woke again and again, sweating and twisting in the darkness. Each time he dropped back into sleep the dream came again until he was forced to leave his soaking bed and sit drinking tea in his kitchen.

Then, just when he thought he was close to a total breakdown – in his research or in his life – the first communication came.

It came in a strangely physical form. He had been expecting something electronic, an email or a video. In the post that morning came a tiny inconsequential envelope, posted in North London. When opened it revealed a scrap of fabric, a long triangular scraping. He 144ecognized the fabric immediately. It was from one of Emily's dresses, a favourite.

I have her, the message said.

Allen waited. There was little he could do. Now he knew the game had commenced, but he had no experience of what to expect.

Do you want her? Do you want to keep her for yourself?

He held his breath at that one, fearing to explode. This was Roger, he knew that. There was no method of reply, just more taunts.

I have her good and deep.

Shopping list for a keepen

Instant mashed potato
Toilet paper
Wet wipes
Cartons juice
Candles
Tea bags
Tissues
Baked beans
Crackers
Margarine
Cheese spread

She prepared meals for him. She made lots of meals for him but usually he didn't want to stay to eat; then after a while, maybe after two years or more, he started to stay with her and sit at the table and eat with her. She remembered thinking every time it was mad, there was no food to make anything with and she hated him and when he was there she hated him being there, but when he wasn't there she wanted him to come down, to talk to her. When she heard him laugh she could imagine her mummy and her friends and maybe that's why she fell in love with him.

She wanted to make a feast, she had been remembering recipes and cooking that she did with her family.

She saved up some tins and waited for him to bring fresh bread. Then she made a feast of bread and mackerels, peaches and custard. She laid it all out on the long table, waiting until the children were sleeping. It was like a wedding feast. She was glad she had married him, because they had two babies and they were doing it like husband and wife all the time. Or all the times he came down to see them. They spent quality time together and sometimes he even stayed overnight. Two times he stayed a whole week, or six days.

146

She didn't know what day it was when he came down and she never knew if he was coming. But one thing she did learn was to know when he was on his way. It took him quite a long time to get from outside down to her level. If she was awake she could hear him start his journey far off. She would run into the dark room and crawl to the back of the space, and from there if she put her ear to the pipes she could hear small sounds echoing in the distance. Sometimes she even thought she could hear people talking and, strangely, children crying and shouting. So that's what's upstairs, she thought. She had a dream about what went on upstairs – maybe his sister lived there with her children and maybe he'd say, 'I have to go and visit my girlfriend,' and his sister would say, 'why don't you bring her back here sometime and introduce her,' and he'd say, 'no, she's shy, I have to go visit her at her house.' And then he'd leave the house and come to his cellar that they didn't know about and climb slowly down into the darkness.

Sometimes she wanted this all to be true and sometimes she hated herself for making up stories about him and what he did up there, because to tell you the truth, it made her even more unhappy. If that was possible.

Only her children were keeping her alive after that.

She said she loved her children a lot and in the end she almost loved the man who kept her here.

She said he brought a woman called Ruth in the seventh year of being down there, company for her. She came to love Ruth, but he took her away again in the ninth year. Ruth helped her look after the children and for a time they had been like sisters, looking out for each other and holding tight through the long, cold nights. But he'd come for her with no warning, soon after the longest, darkest absence. In the eighth year of being down there he had disappeared for six months, or a long time, she wasn't really sure. When he came back, with a scowl and a battering of fists, he pulled Ruth by the wrist and dragged her out of the cellar, never looking back. The children had cried for a long time after that, and a year later they were still unsettled. They were growing fast and coming to an understanding of the environment. It was all they had ever known. She was scared they were becoming golem children who could see in the dark and knew nothing of light.

There were others, but none stayed more than a few weeks, a month at the outside. They came and went, sometimes she didn't even know their names. She stopped getting friendly, understanding that her survival for her children's survival had priority. But priority for what, she began to wonder. She tried not to think that, that thought which had wormed its way into her head in the fifth year had always been kept at bay. How long, how long would she live here? What would happen when she was old? Would her children also grow old down here? Maybe he would make children with her children and the line would continue forever. But of course, he also would, and was, growing old. He was older than her, much older than her. She had started to notice how he had become grey and puffy. His movements were now slower and he had less appetite for that, unlike the early days.

No doubt he could still make new babies with her babies. Not for a few years. And not if she had her way, she would do something to stop it. She started planning in the fifteenth year.

She realised that they were like concentration camp people, at the mercy of their jailers. He could kill us and nobody would care or even know, she thought. At least in the camps they had other people to talk to, maybe a friend or even family or the guards. She imagined that late at night after work they would talk quietly and low in their bunks, even if they were suffused with hunger and worn close to death, they would talk because to talk is human. Isn't it? She had nobody except sometimes other girls and children who stayed for a short time, and they were near useless, they couldn't even talk in English, but she tried, she did try to talk to them. But for many years now, nobody, and the nobody was the worse, the worst.

'He was drugging me,' she said to Emily when they had become used to each other's presence. She was eager to tell her story and Emily listened in resigned horror.

'I know, though he said he wasn't. He called it medicine. "Come for your medicine," he'd say, "you want to stay healthy." He'd bring me medicine every other morning. Then I'd sleep a lot, and when I wasn't sleeping, I'd be stumbling around the space not really having any idea where I was or what was going on. He would still come down for that and we'd fight a bit sometimes. The medicine made me less scared of him and made me forget where I was and what was going on.

'I lost sense of time in those early years, he used to give me medicine a lot of the time and I'd lose any idea of what I was supposed to do. Then he'd come down and tidy up the rooms and sort out the food that I'd dropped or left around and bring me clean clothes. Sometimes he brought me nice clothes.

'The medicine gave me terrible headaches after I woke up.

'I'm not stupid, I grew up down here. I was a child, a baby, when he took me and I forgot a lot about the world and also I didn't know a lot about the world. I knew this was not a normal life and that I was not a normal person. I wanted to know love and to meet people, to enjoy my life. Do you think I'm mad? I have been locked in this basement for years, do you think that sent me mad? I lie awake sometimes and wonder if this is real any more, any more real than up there. And sometimes I don't want to get out because, I know what it is all about down here.

'I have built my own world. I have my five rooms. He is allowed into two of them, that is my rule, not his. Not into the back rooms, they are mine. I made memory things in those back rooms. In three rooms I was safe from him and I built my world. But I had to come out from those rooms to allow myself the privacy of the other three.

'After my first baby was born my life changed. Then I understood love and I knew then that I had to live and escape from him and that. But I also knew that he had a hold over me that was new. He could have snapped my baby like a twig and often I thought that was what he was going to do.

'We didn't do it for two years after my first was born. Then one day he came and he said it is time for this little one to go to the surface and see the sun. And I cried and I fought with him and also it was the only time he came into my back rooms because I hid in there and wouldn't come out. After two days he came in, he didn't say anything, he just came in and I fought him; the only time I fought as hard as I could and I won because he never took my babies.

'Do you want to hear how it is giving birth underground, in the deep dark without your mother or your friends to even know you are going to have a baby? I wasn't happy from the start. I guess I always knew that I could end up with a baby, because of that, it went on for a long time. I asked him for protection, but he wouldn't help me. I wasn't allowed to talk to him, but I wrote him notes telling him that we would end up with a baby and why would he want that. Whatever he wanted for me, I couldn't believe that he wanted more of us in there.

'He did tell me after a while that he wanted more of us. He said that he'd considered catching me a friend, but he'd realised that he could just make more of us. He told me that he'd thought about snatching me a father for my children, for that, you know. So that we'd make babies. But when I asked him what the babies were for, he just went quiet, he couldn't tell me.

'I looked after my babies better than anyone could have done. They never saw the sun. I used to cry for them when they used to cry to me. When they were tiny it didn't seem to matter, but as they grew and learned to crawl and then walk, I found it almost impossible to handle. I so wanted to take them to the beach, to the country. I wanted them to see clouds and cows and the sky. But he said no. He wouldn't even bring them picture books, how wicked is that? The most wicked thing I ever could imagine.

'For ages I thought I could hear a disco pounding away in the night. I never worked out if I could or not, I'd lie in the endless silence trying to focus my ears on the rhythmic, repetitive noise that went on and on and on. It didn't sound like music, but it was like the afterthought of music—what might remain after all the sound in a piece of music had been leeched away by the ground. As the night wore on, I would start to hallucinate; the music was near, the music was the sound of water, I could hear voices along with the music.

'I started to believe that there was a nightclub underground, close to where I was stored, and that if I could pinpoint the source of the noise, I could dig my way through the soil to the club. I used to imagine myself arriving in the club, crashing through the wall onto the dancefloor. Someone would notice a small crack in the wall, a trickle of soil and water, then, as the crack widened, they would look on in horror as fingers grasped through. Suddenly I would push through with one almighty crash, like when the Berlin wall came down. I would fall heroically onto the dance floor. The music would stop, silence as the crowd gathered around this subterranean figure who had fallen into their world. They would press upon me, asking who I was. And I would say, "I'm Abby, I'm Abigail Holden," releasing my true history with one spoken truth. Then the police and ambulance would come and my parents would come with my friends. In later versions of this I carried my two children with me through the tunnel that I dug, the Great Escape. In the tunnel, the Germans are up above, waiting for us to emerge. The air bellows are pumping, I'm rolling through a tunnel on my back with two children strapped to my chest. I told myself I was going to escape.

'No. I don't know if there was ever a nightclub. Was there a club? Is it possible? Did I hear music or was it more of the darkness speaking?

'He told me about how he had built my prison. He told me how he had made traps, terrible traps, that if I tried to escape I would be crushed, that my children would shrivel up and die without me. He told me that a vast concrete block would drop into the passageway. He seemed to like talking about the horrors he had created, that the secrete chambers and the hidden doors and the spikes that would impale me gave him more pleasure than my presence. I don't know if anything he told me is real but it is in my head. It is my life.

'He talked to me with silence. I learned to hear what he was saying in that silence. After a long time, our relationship became so close that we understood each other without words. Not that I came to accept the situation, but I must admit I forgot another life. Partly I did that on purpose, I would not allow the life I had before to exist anymore. I could not allow myself to think about my mother and my father and my sisters and my brother. To do this, to dwell on what they might be doing now, would have finished me off.

'I lost track of how much time had passed, so it was not so hard to deliberately lose track of who I was and who I had been. It is very hard to track time in darkness with no human contact. For many years he never let me have a clock, nor a light that I could control. I didn't have hot water for more time than that – I had forgotten things that you know every day. How to wash my hair, how to take a bath to clean away the sweat of the day. I forgot the seasons and the weather. I grew older, my body changed, but I knew nothing of the world upside, only of my filthy, dark space.

'I felt I was going insane, losing my mind. For a long while I was sure that was the best thing, that I should forget that I was human and in that way peace would come. But it never quite did, I always woke with perfect knowledge of who I was and how I had got here. And I always went to sleep knowing that I had no way out.

'You see, he built his dungeon and I performed in it. It was an act, an act like an actor would perform. He never asked for performance, but over the years I came to realise the roles we were playing. Then I tried many ways to make it into theatre, to leave my body while in that place. But I never quite found the trick. I was always present. His demands got harder to do over the years and I got weaker in my body and in my mind, I thought. In that place I could see how he would eventually kill me.

'But it never came to pass, he never finished me off. I could not work out what the endgame was, but I had accepted that my life was to stay in this hole and be buried there at the appropriate time. I worried more about my children. I could accept what would happen to me, but not what would happen to them. And would it go further.

'It was a hard time.

'I have to find a way to pass the time. Time changes, it moves faster or slower, depending on things.

'You'd probably think that time in here has passed very slowly, that I spend every day in a state of boredom, waiting for it to end. But it doesn't work like that – the time here has passed very quickly. I've taken to imagining that I'm not producing any memories. If you asked me straight out what happened last week, last month, or for the last year, I couldn't begin to tell you. I made a memory machine for that, because I wanted to tell people what happened in here.'

She took Emily by the hand and led her into the darkest of the dark back rooms and showed her the piles of tiny scrap dolls, the markers of the months and years in this place.

'If you asked me to guess how long I've been in here, I might answer, just a few months. If I think back to the beginning, it seems like a few months ago. In between is a lot of greyness, for sure. And my babies were born and have grown up, so I know that years have passed. And there is him, he comes regularly.'

Emily finally understood the hopeless, helpless mass in that room and how the years had passed here and her heart broke again.

I'm not stupid, I knew from the beginning that I would get babies. Well, at the start I believed that I would get out, that he would let me free and I would run home and cry to my mother about what had happened and there would be lots of police and then a court case and then I would go back to school. And I would have stories to tell.

Or he would kill me. I used to lie awake at night thinking about how he would murder me and trying to imagine how it might happen. I used to wonder whether he would tell me before he did it, or whether he would grab me suddenly while doing something else (it, probably), and strangle me in quick motion. And what I would feel and think while it happened, and whether I would know I was going. And of course, I wondered what I would find afterwards, would I wake up in heaven or in some black pit? Maybe in hell, as I'd been doing some very bad things.

That was before I got snatched myself. One minute I was walking home, singing to myself as it was dark and a bit scary. Then this guy asked me something, where was something, I couldn't quite hear him. He was standing next to a van, but I never thought for a moment. I don't remember anything about what he did, but I woke up in his van feeling sick. Then I threw up.

Before I was taken, I never thought much about those hostages in Beirut that everyone used to go on about. I've thought a lot about them over the years. They spent years in holes in the ground, chained to radiators, and they never knew when they'd be let out. But they knew why they were there. Somehow, they did better than me, I think. The whole world waited for them to come home again. I don't think anyone has been waiting for me to come home. Sometimes I imagine my funeral, everyone crying. But they wouldn't have known what happened. They wouldn't have had any idea that I was still alive under their feet.

He said he liked me because I was smart and that I knew something about the world. But apart from that he didn't say that much to me. At least for a few years, must have been about four, he didn't really talk to me at all. And he didn't tell me anything about the world. I didn't ask him either. I couldn't bring myself to ask him: what can you ask someone who has taken you off the street and locked you in a cellar? You think they are mad and that they probably don't care much for the world. He used to come down and leave food and then that.

I spent a lot of time imagining what his life was like up there. I was down there and he was up there. I tried to imagine where I was. I didn't know, but I invented Edinburgh, as I'd been there for a school trip the year before and we'd been down the underworld of the city on a guided tour, so I had some idea that there was an underground in that city. Because, being a girl like all other girls, apart from being scared by horror videos I hadn't given much thought to the underground of the city. I sort of knew that London was filled with tunnels lost and hidden and that there must be a lot of underground stuff that was lost. But I didn't have any reason to think about it.

But I did think a lot about who he was and what he did when he was upstairs. Whether he lived on his own or with someone else, and whether anyone else knew about me. I guessed that no-one would have any idea, because who would let a young girl waste away underground in such horrible circumstances for so long? But then maybe that was how they got their kicks, he came down for that, then went back up and told his story.

One morning Emily noticed that the children were cupping their ears to the side of their heads as if listening to some distant sound, something she could not hear. She cupped her own hand to her ear, straining in the dark to make something out. The only sounds she heard were their own footsteps and the distant dripping of water. She could not discern anything new and wondered if they were playing some sort of game.

Then she heard it. Scrape, scrape, tap. Almost inaudible, distant, remote. She looked at the children and they shook their heads at her, concern in their eyes.

'Is coming.'

'Who?'

'His. Him. Uncle. Ars father.'

The hairs instantly stood up on the back of her neck. She concentrated in the dark, trying to make out what they were hearing. There was the whirr of a fan somewhere far off, the air system. It wasn't always on but now she could taste the fresh air it brought. Then, in the deep far distance, almost imperceptible, she discerned the tiniest clang and then the echoing of feet on something hard. Barely, scraping sounds. She tried so hard to hear that her mind started to confuse vision and sound and, in the darkness, small snippets of light whirled around her head. As she pressed her forehead in concentration, she heard small scrapings while her eyes saw swirling clouds of starlings flocking around her head. The scrapings disengaged themselves from the background noises and suddenly became obvious.

She found she was sweating and felt her eyes bulging, terror swept over her, her limbs became limp. Now she could hear it clearly. It was the sound of somebody making their way, painfully, slowly, down into the space, maybe crawling, maybe dragging something, she could not be sure. It seemed to go on for hours but was really only a short period which she spent tensed and frozen, immobile, waiting. Waiting.

Then, across on the other side of the space, the wall cracked and allowed a sliver of golden light to describe a thin line upon the wall. The first light she had seen for days. As she watched in wonder, it widened. A door was pushed open allowing a line of light to fall forward upon the floor.

A shadow emerged from a hole in the wall and light flooded the cellar, burning Emily's eyes. The shape unfolded itself and rose up into a large man. It reached behind itself and flicked a switch. Full, harsh, unyielding light flooded the space, blinding her. She shut her eyes tight and tried to blink away the pain.

Then, although Emily felt terror, it was a strange terror, she knew from the stories of the children, and their hidden mother, that death wasn't the plan. Her captor wasn't a murderer, at least not in the ordinary way. She felt a different kind of terror, not a fear of death but an overwhelming helplessness, a horror that entered her body, crept through her muscles and into her bones and settled there, reminding her that she was a prisoner.

Whatever happens now, she thought, nobody will know. And it is planned, has been planned.

The man emerged into the space and he walked calmly across to stand in front of her, grinning. He was tall and broad, well dressed in a suit and tie. She noticed his large freckled hands and short hair. He continued to smile at her. She didn't expect this, didn't know how to respond. He was not a raving lunatic, not some crippled or dribbling monster, but a broad-faced man dressed in a good suit.

'Hello,' he said. 'How are you feeling?'

'Let me the fuck out of here.'

Then without warning or decision or control Emily found herself jumping off the bed and flinging herself directly onto him, trying to strike his face with her fists. The big man pushed her easily away and didn't stop grinning. He balled up a fist and punched her full in the face.

The unexpectedness and suddenness of the strike sent her spinning across the room, onto the hard concrete floor. She'd never been hit in this way and the pain was huge, but it was the metallic taste of blood and the shock of an uncaring fist that caused the first tears to flow.

Afterwards, Emily asked Abby why she had never killed him. It shocked her to hear herself ask. The thought came from no-where, but as soon as she said it, she knew they could do it.

'At first, when I was little, there was nothing I could do. He is a big man, as you have seen. Then there were children. I did think of it, but I thought he never tried to kill me so why? He told me I would never get out, I believed him.' She tailed off, uncertainly.

'Didn't you think, one day, maybe he'd let you go?'

'If I was nice to him? If I looked after his children? I was always nice to him, as much as I could, but he told me about the terrible traps. I don't think there's any way out, even if he is dead. If he dies, it just gets worse.'

She seemed resigned, as if any thoughts of getting out had long died in her. But Emily wanted to get out, knew that there was a world out there still waiting for her. Fuck traps, she suddenly thought, they are probably all a lie in the way that everything in this crazy place is a lie.

'We're going to die in here anyway, if we don't do something. Have you thought about it, what happens to him, he won't live for ever, he's an old man? Getting older.'

She steeled herself. This isn't what I do, she thought. A knife being pushed into human flesh, it held horrors. It is what Allen would do, she thought, and what he would want me to do. How do I get a knife, can I fashion one from the cutlery? Thoughts of prisoner of war films came to her, they were imaginative, they made what they needed to escape.

Sharpen something on the wall, make a sharpie, a shiv and push it into his ribs, she thought, the ideas suddenly thrilling her.

'I'm not scared of him,' she said.

'I have something,' Abby said. 'I made it, a long time ago, for our food, for cutting. Now you are here, I'm not afraid anymore either. You will do it, for my children.'

She started crying and Emily reached out and held her close.

The Collector

Allen found he was writing more. He wrote late into the night, avoiding the dark silence for as long as he could. He was in demand. After his return from Belgrade and the disappearance of Emily he had become the first port of call every time someone went missing, a useful talking head for television and an authority on strange vanishings. His friends in the police continued to regard him with some suspicion, but still came to him occasionally for information or advice. He felt himself elevated above the fray. The temper he'd fallen into started to dissipate.

Out of a sense of duty he kept in touch with Emily's mother, making a sort of uneasy peace out of their shared misery. She had long realised that the stories the police had whispered to the papers and which they had gleefully repeated were nonsense. There were no other relationships, she hadn't been seeing a teacher or a retired detective, she hadn't been seen with a famous musician and she certainly hadn't run off with a pupil. They had both learned a lot about the cruelties of the English press during that time and it had changed both of them. From that a sort of accommodation had been reached, an understanding that they were both suffering and neither was to blame.

'Maybe she just had enough of me,' he said, unwilling to share his true thoughts about her fate. He could only leave her in a sort of mindless void between thinking he had done it and his deepest nightmares about what might be happening to her daughter. They sat in long silences, utterly unsure of how to talk about her.

'They are doing something,' he said, but he knew the trail had gone completely cold.

Maybe, maybe in years to come, if things changed, he'd get a message. He could hardly bear to think about it.

He understood she wasn't dead; he knew she'd been taken. There was nothing he could say or do. She was with Roger. There was no body, but this didn't mean she was still alive, or dead. He just knew she was alive. It was the way. He knew how this worked. If she had been killed, he would know.

Emily was part of Roger's plan for him, part of the learning curve. Maybe taking and keeping wasn't enough, maybe in the end it was important for outsiders to understand, to experience the exquisite torture of long-term holding. He tried not to think about it. In the night he'd try any trick to stop his mind building pictures of Emily in a huge black unheated basement. It was hard to stop the images coming.

He spent long evenings watching trash television, drinking red wine, trying to ward off the thoughts and drifting into a void. Looking for distraction he pulled out a book he'd picked up in Roger's flat which had been in his bag since his return. He remembered it now, *The Collector*. It was a story about taking. It seemed strange to him that someone like Roger would be interested in reading such a thing, but he flipped the book open. As usual, as he read, he found himself drifting quickly into sleep. And as he slept, the same dream came again and again, descent, darkness, disorientation. In the dream he was a boy again. He had crossed the road from his parents' house and entered the house opposite, the house that had scared and tormented him as a child, and he found there was a staircase that ran both up and down, around a square well. He leaned on the banister and looked over, into a dark, deep, space where there should not be a basement, and he knew he must not go down while knowing, even in the dream, that he would go down. Fear overtook him but still he could not leave and still he could not surface.

When, eventually, he woke up, the book had fallen to the floor beside him and lay splayed open on the carpet. As he picked it up, he saw an address written in spidery elegant hand-writing inside the back cover. He stared at it for a moment, wondering why it was there and then it came to him. It must be Roger's London address. Had to be. I've got your fucking address, he thought, and I'm coming to get you. A deep, shuddering fear swept through him.

Hampstead

When first light came, not wanting to waste another moment, he pulled on some clothes and ran to the tube. He exited at Hampstead and climbed up and up above London where the houses got bigger and grander.

He soon found Marsham Street – it had a lot of big houses and a lot of trees. Many of the houses converted into flats, not all of them exactly salubrious but not grubby either. Money. Security. Safety, he thought. Some were recent conversions, smart with tidy bricked-over front drives and video cameras on the doors, architect extensions with concrete and glass, stainless steel and bleached wood. The older conversions looked like long-term tenancies, lots of poured concrete, lumpen extensions, overgrown front gardens with somewhat worn-out cars jammed into them.

And then, the house he was after, the address in the book he'd somehow brought from Roger's. Though it was only a couple of streets away from some of the smartest streets in the capital, it looked tired and isolated, though it was probably the most valuable plot in the street.

He stared up at the building, embedded in the side of a hill. A garden behind a high wall dropped away to the south of the building. The people who live on the hill, he thought. This was the sort of house that people would crave, with a location to die for. The trees were huge and heavy, shutting out light to the sloping garden, ignored, unpruned for many years. He wanted to look over the fence, to peer into the space beyond, but something held him back. Not here, not in this street. Not with respectable people watching over his movements. He could feel them watching him though the street seemed silent and deserted.

Climbing fifteen steps to the front door, Allen wondered what he would say. He didn't relish meeting Roger on the doorstep. Stepping quickly into the tiled entranceway, he reached up to the large front door and rang the bell. His heart began to beat faster. His mind emptied. He knew he was winging it, his mouth went dry and, as he heard footsteps on a wooden floor behind the huge door, he drew breath. Someone peered through the coloured glass at him, then he could hear them twisting at a heavy door handle.

A small woman opened the door and he exhaled.

'Hello,' he said with a forced smile. 'My name's Allen Kimbo.' He held out his hand but she looked right through it. 'I'm looking for Roger.'

The woman stared at him for a long moment, pointedly ignoring his hand. She was dressed in a flowery housecoat and slippers,

'Have you come about the flat?' she said. His mind went blank, then in a flash he grasped what she meant. She was so natural and so straightforward that, in fear of derailing her, he just nodded enthusiastically.

'Yes, yes.' His breath became faster again, now. He couldn't believe she was going to invite him in like this. 'I'll just get the keys,' she said. 'You'll have to let yourself in. Roger is not here and I'm afraid I never go down there. You understand, don't you?'

A note of self-protective sympathy crept into her voice. Confused, Allen reached out to take the keys she had unhooked from behind the door.

'And?' he asked, raising an eyebrow.

'Oh, it's down there,' she said, vaguely gesturing to the side of the house. 'Just follow the path round and you'll find a green door at the back.'

He swung the keys gently and stepped back down to find the path. There was a big flat built under the main house. It looked backwards, away from the road. A thin path led round to the front door below the east side. There was a small garden, not even that really, just a yard contained within a wooden fence that separated it from a large, sloping city garden. The ground dropped away steeply from the flat, down to the backs of the houses on the road below. The road that the house sat on curled around the west end of the house and itself dropped down to join the next road. A small gate provided an entrance from the road to what seemed to be the garden of the house, although this space was overgrown and dark.

He felt the weight of the key in his hand, an old-fashioned mortice lock key with a large tang. When he got to the door, Allen slotted the key neatly into the lock and it turned with a satisfying, oily click. A second lock up above was similarly easily opened and Allen stepped through the front door and into a narrow, dim hallway. He realised that he wasn't breathing, that he was frightened to be in a space below Roger's house. Suddenly lightheaded, he walked quickly down the corridor and into the living room. Bracing himself on the windowsill, Allen took deep breaths while looking across at the lower gardens.

Abigail

Sometimes he came down and took loads of photos with a little camera, Abigail told Emily. For the early years, although he didn't talk to me or bring me anything much like clothes or books or anything, he was the only human I knew, and I came to look forward to him visiting. Even though I knew that would happen when he came, even that became part of my life in a way that you won't understand.

By your reaction to that I can feel that you will start to hate me. If you know what happened down here and what it meant to me, you'll start to hate me because you won't be able to handle it. So, I'm keeping it to myself. I was girl stuck in a hole with a monster. What happened to me was my life for a long time, and I made it my life. You didn't come to find me, you didn't dig through the walls and pull me out.

For a long time I had dreams about being rescued. I thought for sure my dad would work out who was keeping me and would come and dig down in the night and pull me to freedom through a hole in the wall. Sometimes I dreamed this rescue in such detail that I would wake up and wonder how I was still down here.

At the start of my time here I didn't know the rules or even if there were any rules, so I used to shout at him or ask him for things. The first time I talked to him, he punched me. I'd never been hit before by anyone. I remember the shock of it, the jarring crunch as his closed fist whacked into my face. It wasn't really the pain but the unexpected shock of it, like I'd just walked into a lamp-post while looking in the other direction, if you've ever done that. The moment it happens, like you are just wondering what this thing is that materialized from nowhere to wallop me in the mouth. After that, I was on my guard when he was down, always thinking that if I looked away a post might appear out of nowhere and whack me one and break another tooth and split my lip and spew red blood all down my front.

I'd never been hit, I'd lived a very quiet life, but I had walked into a post once, so I knew the feeling. I was a kid really. I knew nothing about violence and control or about sex, though I'd thought about it, we all did. My friends and I used to talk about doing it, but we hadn't done it.

I learned the rules and I only talked to him by writing notes. We didn't have much of a relationship.

Not that we ever did, really. What came later, you couldn't describe it as a relationship. But it became something.

I'm not going to talk about that.

At the very start I thought he'd torture me and then kill me. I'd been watching horror films with my friends.

At first there was one book down here, so I read that book again and again. It was not a very nice book, but it wasn't really a horror book like we passed around at school. It was feeble. That girl in it would never act like that, all arty and clever. She'd be so scared she'd wet herself and also that he would never be like that, like he'd want to rape her on the first night. Then he'd probably get a huge knife and stab her to death when he found out she didn't love him.

Like I said, I read that book so many times I know most of it backwards. In my head I wrote my own version of it, where it was me in the cellar. What I would do. Different.

Although I was not allowed to talk to him, he talked to me. One day he took me upstairs and out into the world.

You might ask how he could take an abducted girl out of the cellar that he makes her live in and out into the world. Why didn't I scream and run away? Well, it was about eight years after he got hold of me and by then I was not the person I had started life as. It became crucial to my survival, before I got my children, that I wasn't connected to Abby before the start. Abby before he caught me. I would not allow myself to make any connection with that life I had left behind. If I found myself trying to remember things from my previous life I had to stop immediately. Then I could continue, but only on the basis that it was someone else I was thinking about. The things I remembered had happened to someone else.

Below

Fifty minutes passed before she realised that the man she had sent down to the flat hadn't come back up. He might just have left, she thought, after seeing the flat. But he had the key. Her husband would be angry if he'd gone off with it and she hadn't even asked his name. She didn't want to upset him, he'd been calmer since he retired and she worked hard to keep it that way.

They'd had some bad tenants down there, although her husband had always dealt with them. Treat them harsh, he said. If you give them an inch, they take a mile. It had never really been any of her business and she'd never intervened. She'd really prefer not to let the flat, it wasn't as if they needed the money, Roger's pension was more than adequate and the money from her parents' house could provide any luxuries they needed. But it was his house, she supposed, since he was the one who'd inherited it. It had made a lovely family house, and they'd been very lucky to live right up here on the hill. It had made her feel privileged, even when they were young. It had made-up to some degree for a husband who didn't pay her much attention and who had his own interests, his own life, almost.

Her husband walked up the hill slowly, heavily. He hadn't expected to be back so early but his meeting with an old friend had been unexpectedly cancelled. He hadn't found out until he arrived. Now he was upset and grumpy. How could people be so hopeless? His breathing was heavy as he strained to reach the top of the hill. He thought again about selling up, about moving to a bungalow by the coast. Maybe it was time.

He turned into the garden, unlatching and then latching the gate behind him. His step was hardly light though he had few cares in the world. Everything was going well. Retirement suited him, it gave him more time for his hobbies. Except for his wife. He wasn't really so happy to see more of her, but he kept himself busy and out of her way and she out of his. Damned wives, sometimes they didn't really conform to type. Now she wanted to go off cruising in Norway, the fjords or some such, but he had things to look after. It was a busy time. Years of effort had paid out, now he wanted the rewards. They were destined to spend their declining days together yet apart. He knew that was the best he could expect.

When he reached the house the front door was ajar, another of her annoying habits, as if there was no danger in this part of London. He certainly didn't feel safe. He hated the insecure and insincere way her attitude came across – he preferred locked doors and locked emotions.

She stood in the hallway, tea towel in hand, wringing it nervously. She smiled. 'Hello.'

He nodded at her, sweat beading his forehead. Then he looked at her again. 'What's wrong?' he asked.

'A man came to look at the flat,' she said. 'I gave him the key, sent him down.'

'And?' he said.

'He hasn't come back. I'm afraid he might have gone off with it.'

'Don't worry, my dear,' he said. 'I'll take a look.' He made his way quickly out of the house again.

The basement flat was accessed by a side gate. He quickly unlocked the door and strode around, getting the measure of it. Nice place to live, Allen thought, wondering what the fuck he was doing here. If this was Roger's house, then there must be some connection between this place and Emily. But not this neat and tidy and altogether elegant and light-filled flat. This wasn't a place for keepen.

Two small bedrooms. A kitchen with a very small window directly under the entrance of the house above, a scullery with an old-fashioned screened window and then a large living room with a window that overlooked the hillside. Nothing here. Nothing that led anywhere. The flat had that strange odour of neglect, he thought. Maybe some cheap air freshener.

The air was stale. He looked at small drifts of dust on the windowsills and tried to imagine what had been placed there until not so long ago. Time slowed and he edged around the space, looking at fragments of tack that had held pictures to walls, pin holes, dust in corners, grime on windows. The place was clean but not immaculate. It was strange how a life had been removed, expunged. He ran his fingers along the edge of the sink and sniffed the air again.

He realised he was listening to something, a sound he knew. A very low bass hum in the distance, something he'd heard before. He struggled to place it, to attach a noise to some re-membered event, but the harder he tried, the further the thrum drifted into the background until it was as if the very effort of trying to hear it drowned it out. He stopped thinking about it and the sound returned.

He closed his eyes and swayed on the balls of his feet and as he did so it came to him. An air pump, he thought. Circulating air. But not in here, in here there is no air circulating. It's down. Below me. In the floor. Allen lay down full length on his side and put his ear to the floor. Then stood up, and down again.

He lay for a while, a cheek pressed against the grubby beige carpet, holding his breath. He moved forward and then, raising himself to a semi-crawling position, he scuttled across the room to the corner and lay down again full length. Now he could hear it. He thumped on the floor with his fist. Concrete. Then he kicked down with his foot. Floorboards.

He reached out and gripped the edge of the carpet. With a loud rip it came partly away in his hands. He pulled at the under-lay to reveal unbroken concrete screed. He scrabbled at the edges of the screed, pulling at a wooden edging but nothing would come loose. When he stood up the humming stopped but when he put his ear back to the floor he could hear it clearly. He looked around for something to bang with, but the flat was empty. Eventually he found a stick next to the back door and, walking around the flat, he banged the end of it on the carpet. In the kitchen the floor was lino. The floor here sounded different, it reverberated, slightly hollow. Drop, ding. Drop, ding. Drop, thud. He tore at the edge of the covering and ripped pieces out until the floor underneath was revealed and there at the side of the room, hard up against the wall, a clear rectangular shape, a different texture to the rest of the floor.

He went to the window and pulled it open. Looking out he noticed there was a small window set into the wall just above the ground, and jutting out from that window, the outlet of an air vent.

Abigail

I worked out the size of my prison. I made a plan of it in my head. I could draw it for you now. I memorised it on purpose in the first few months, so that if I was rescued I would be a good witness. Where did these things happen, was it in the first room or the side room? Or the back room. Which room was the bed in? Where did the water leak in? Where were the light switches? How many cupboards were there?

I paced the space and measured it all in foot spaces. Sometimes I did this in the dark, sometimes in the light, when he let it be on. I learned not to fear the dark, not to imagine anything else in there with me. Just me, being me, born anew into this dark place, my world.

I didn't try to remember anything, certainly not my family and my friends. Or the sky and the sun and the rain. Or the sea and the beach. Or my dog, or my rabbits. They all moved into a huge grey hole that was called *thentime*, and which I could not think about.

It's quite easy when you work on it to close off part of your life if you want to survive. The truth is, I did start to forget all that stuff and I didn't want to think about it. And I did become me and not Abigail.

Anyway, after a time I did start to believe that I wasn't Abigail, that I was someone else. I didn't know who I was.

I think he drugged me. What am I saying, I know he drugged me. He drugged me and he raped me again and again and again. I never had a chance to make any sort of decision about what happened.

Sometimes he brought me books and newspaper cuttings, magazine articles, about people abducted and forced to live underground for whatever reason. He intended to scare me, but I relished the reading material and these real stories of real people never frightened me – it was only the story of myself that had the power to scare me.

I was isolated in the way those people were isolated: locked in underground chambers on the whim of a powerful autocrat whose word was law. But he didn't have a scurrying team of helpers who had convinced themselves that this had to be done. With us there was only me and him, me down here and him up there.

I long remembered that last day of sunlight, though I knew that over time my memory had been replaced by a memory of a memory and the sunlight I remembered had become a memory of sunlight.

I wasn't scared much and the sex wasn't a problem. Well, let's put that a different way. The first year was very scary, there wasn't a day really that didn't contain horror. But that was because I didn't understand how things would work and what might happen next. You can't be afraid of what you know. Being stuck in a cellar with no light, with rooms full of things that you can't see, and waiting, always waiting, for a monster to come back down. That's fear and that's horror. But even that first year got better as it went on. I realised that not every day was going to be bad. After a while you can't sustain the fear, you just can't.

The sex was another thing. I got used to that after a while. I never got to like him and the first two years were very bad. But you have to remember I was a thirteen-year-old girl, I'd never had a boyfriend and even if I had nothing would have happened.

Everyone wants to know when it started. And they have their ideas about what might have gone on. But I can tell you, the sex started on the first day. It was the whole idea of taking me, of locking me up. Even I could see that, and I was a baby. I knew what sex was, I wasn't stupid, but I never had to think much about it for myself. Until that day. But it did start on the first day and it went on and on while he was around. Then there was a lot of time when he wasn't around, so I'd sort of forget about it all.

I never thought about babies. I didn't have my periods for the first year. Then they came, and obviously he and I both thought about babies. He wouldn't use the johnnies mostly and I didn't think I could get a baby from this man that I hated. Looking back, I know he wanted a baby. A baby for his baby. And pretty soon he got one, there wasn't much I could do about that. Of course, my baby, my babies, they are what saved me in the end. He didn't care while they were little, he left us alone. I had to look after them alone. I'd had them alone, in this hole, on my own, so looking after them was easy. And he did feed us, I'll give him that. He is a provider.

I used to lie in the dark and dream of my friends in the up world, what were they doing. And the sex, I'm sorry to admit it, but I thought a lot about sex. Not as something that happened to me. What happened to me was conditioning and punishment, breaking in, like a wild horse from the prairies. I wondered what had become of my friends and their boyfriends. Whether Tracy had gone all the way with Freddie. Whose mother had read their diaries. I used to wonder about what they would think of me now, if they knew how I'd ended up. My thoughts were stalled at a stage when I had friends and dreams. But that life was not my life, it was a fantasy that I could use to keep myself entertained. It was a Disney film or a big fat book on a rainy day, not memories of a life that I used to have. Because after the event I didn't have any life.

Just him coming to fuck me night after night. Him and his beard and his ideas.

After she had listened for what seemed like hours to the process of slowly escalating sounds, of somebody descending through a deep and hidden passageway, and the tension in the basement got tighter and tighter until she thought she might scream, the steel door crashed open. Emily sat on her haunches and took deep breaths, willing her heart to slow down. Through the gloom the man emerged again. Emily stared at the shadow he formed as it advanced into the space until it stood in front of her.

She could barely see him in the dark, the low watt bulb cast strange, disconcerting shadows into the corners. The air was thick with moisture. She stared at him with wide eyes, willing herself to stay still. Behind Emily, through a metal grill, another face, white and immobile, watched him, unblinking.

Emily stared with the slightest smile on her face. She didn't move, she clenched her hands into fists at her sides until the knuckles whitened. Inside her, her heart still beat furiously.

'My boyfriend will kill you. He will find you and he will get us out of here and he will kill you,' she whispered to him. Then the tears came freely, flowing from her as she realised the futility of that statement, the fact that Allen could be anywhere, she could be anywhere, he would never find out where she was kept.

He extended his arm from the elbow towards Emily. 'Stand up,' he said. She got slowly to her feet, keeping her eyes fixed on his. He shuffled half a step forward.

'We've been together a long time, me and her, and I'm in her power,' he said. 'She doesn't want to return to the surface. She doesn't want you interfering. She has no ability to function up there. She has a life down here, a family, she wants for nothing.'

'She was taken when she was a child. You took her.'

'She loves me as a father and as a husband,' he said, taking another small step forward. Emily took a step sideways.

She swayed; the man blinked hard. This is it, she thought.

He stepped forward with unexpected speed and grasped her hands, pulling her towards him. 'Stop,' she screamed as he tugged at her.

As if her scream was a signal, in the blackness behind them a door clicked softly and a shadow emerged, fluttering as if dancing. It approached and performed a strange, ritualistic movement in front of Roger, flitting left then right, moving so fast in the half-light that they could not follow the movements of this sparrow figure. Like a film projected at the wrong speed, the wraith, jerky in the half silver light, shadow-fluttered over him, stepped to him, over him, onto him, reached out and touched him and then, with the lightness of air, floated away back into the darkness. The man let go of Emily and she fell backwards onto the floor.

He stood still for a long moment then reached for his chest and made a series of small gasping sounds, sicked up a long, thin stream of vomit, and fell backwards onto the floor. He made no further noise but lay full length in the shadows. Emily could see his feet in the pale puddle of light that a small bulb cast. Apart from that the place was in darkness. The gloom seemed to settle tighter around her. She turned. She could not locate Abigail but could hear the children crying in the distant darkness.

Emily walked confidently to the cell door and yanked it open. From inside the small, white-faced family, the children and the ghost of their mother, looked up at her in wonder.

She looked at the woman. 'We did it. What now?'

There was no reply, just silence and the realisation that she was locked in with a family of spectres and a corpse.

Exeat

The call came through at 11:18 precisely in the morning, routed by the emergency number operators to West Hampstead police station.

'Police.'

'My name is Mrs Standen. I live at 37 Chilcot Road. My nephew has gone missing.'

The person who had answered the phone was bored. The last thing she needed was a dotty old lady with a missing nephew. After taking a full name and address she asked, 'How old is your nephew.'

'He's fifty-two,' Mrs Standen said.

'Could you tell me why you think he's gone missing?'

Mrs Standen was pretty sure. 'Because he didn't come back. He went to feed his snakes last night. He does every night, and I know it sounds a bit funny, but he really does love those lizards. I don't like them at all, I have told him many times I won't feed them when he's not there, but he says he has it all under control. Anyway, he went down last night to feed them and he hasn't come back. I've just checked his room and it doesn't look like he ever came back in. And now I'm worried.'

'Where does he keep them?' the controller asked.

'Down in the cellar, of course,' Mrs Standen said.

'Look, I'll pass it on to a car. Ask them to drop by and have a look around. It won't be very quick. But they'll be there as soon as they can.'

To the old woman, the PCs who eventually turned up at her door looked about fifteen. By that time, though, she had worked herself up into a frenzy of fear and anticipation. Her nephew hadn't returned, and this behaviour was so unlikely that she suspected the worst. He did travel abroad, sometimes for long periods, but he never, never left the house without telling her. In fact, he never did anything without making sure she knew where he was. He had no vices that she knew of, except those darned lizards, which she considered an abomination. He spent a lot of time on them, too much, she considered. Still, he did look after her and provided company in her old age. He was a good boy, really. She told herself not to burst into tears again, that these police officers would find him. Maybe he'd had a funny turn. Maybe he'd slipped and hurt himself and couldn't climb back up the stairs.

'He keeps creatures,' she said, 'down in the cellar.' Come in, come in. She led them through the large house, towards the back. 'There's a staircase here,' she said, pointing to a wooden door at the end of a corridor. The woman police officer opened the latch. There was no lock. She peered in, looking for a light switch.

'When did you say he went down there?' she asked.

'About seven o'clock last night,' Mrs Standen said. 'He always goes down around that time, it's his hobby.'

'And you haven't been down, to have a look?'

'I never go down there,' the old woman said. 'I don't like the dark and I certainly don't like snakes.'

The officers made their way down. There was a light and a steep staircase that wound its way down past a basement room which contained hundreds of cardboard boxes and into a sub-basement below that. Now they were far under the house, deep in the London clay. The lower basement was divided into two equal-sized rooms. One was a built-in workshop with work-benches and saws, a pillar drill, vices and multiple racking systems. The second was a storeroom which contained shelving on which was stacked a variety of packaged food and plastic containers.

The two police officers looked at each other and smiled. There were no reptiles, no snakes or lizards. No cages, nothing that would indicate such a hobby, nothing that fitted the woman's description of why her nephew spent time in the cellar. The WPC raised an eyebrow and smiled. 'He's up to something he doesn't want his aunt to know about.'

'Either that, or she's not well,' her partner said.

The continued to walk slowly around the room, lifting a few items and shoving boxes aside. There was really nothing to search, nowhere else to examine. Now they convinced themselves that this was a fool's errand. Whatever was going on in this household, whether or not someone was missing, this basement didn't seem to offer a solution. They drifted back through to the workshop and onto the staircase. As the policewoman stepped onto the first tread they thought they heard a noise, a slight *clang* which emanated somewhere in the depths of the space, somewhere off behind them. They both froze, silent, waiting to see whether it repeated.

'Did you ...' the leading officer said. And then they heard another, softer sound. They both turned and looked back into the space they were vacating, and through into the storeroom. Some notion from their training, some idea that you should discount the obvious, believe the unlikely, came to mind and they dismounted the staircase and, walking slowly and carefully, both re-entered the second space and walked slowly around it in opposite directions.

'What do you think that was?'

'Probably nothing.'

He moved a container on a shelf and looked behind it. She stared at the ceiling, then at the floor. She sniffed. 'Can you smell something, something stale, a bit rank?'

He sniffed ostentatiously. 'Maybe. Not sure.' The room itself smelled of underground spaces.

They continued their circumnavigation. He tapped the floor with his foot.

She opened a cupboard. Ropes. She opened the next. Sanitary towels. She eyed the dusty floor.

'Oh, come on, nothing here,' he said. They turned again and *clang*. Louder this time, unignorable.

'What the fuck,' she said. They held their breath, motionless, willing their ears to pick up more sound. 'Behind those shelves,' he said. They both took a couple of steps forward and grasped the end shelving unit, trying to pull it forward. It didn't budge, it seemed to be attached to the wall, as if with springs. They pulled, then stopped, then she reached under a shelf and tried to lift it and the entire unit moved upwards, away from the wall. Hinged like a garage door, it swung upwards and upwards until it rested parallel to the ceiling. They stared at it in amazement, then slowly lowered their gaze to the wall which had a rough opening through brickwork into the darkness beyond.

Climbing out of the window and dropping down into the grass, Allen looked quickly around for a tool. He found a fencing post in the long grass and he held it full length above his head as a battering tool.

The window frame was heavy, old-fashioned, properly constructed wood. A piece of work, he thought, a proper piece of work. He hit it, then again and again until it splintered, breaking away from the surrounding stonework. He smashed it out piece by piece, opening up a small dark hole in the wall almost level with the ground. Allen stuck his head in. He'd done this before. It was an entrance to something, some sort of space under the house. He wasn't sure quite what. The trick now was to get in as quickly as possible. He pushed himself in head first, not caring about the jagged edges to the hole he'd created, and, dropping onto outstretched arms, he fell and rolled forward into the darkness. He sat up and looked around. He was in a short corridor. To his right a wooden door would lead back outside and right in front of him, a heavy wooden door right under the house. This is it. The thought swept clammy sweat through his body immediately. This is a fucking hole hidden under his house in the middle of London. And I found it. Breathing deeply, he reached for the handle and pulled but the door was locked. A wave of claustrophobia swept over him. He started to sweat wildly.

Out of nowhere a voice came back to him, the sergeant shouting.

Get in there, you stupid. cowardly cunt. Get your stupid arse in there.

The blackness reared in front of him. The dank dark smell washed over him.

But sarge, there are people in there. Bodies in there. Something bad has happened. Blood in there.

Get in there, you dumb moron, get in there before I smash your stupid arse.

They are moving in there. Moaning.

Pushing his back against the wall behind him, Allen lifted a leg and kicked solidly against the door. One... Two... Three... and it started to go. Four... Five... and the door flew open and a damp, acrid cloud flew out and enveloped him, catching at the back of his throat and making him cough wildly. A shaft of light from the window behind him illuminated millions of fragments of dust. He breathed the stale air and looked into the space. A large, dry cellar stretched back under the house.

'Emily,' he shouted. 'Emily.' There was silence in the space. He could see a dust-covered workbench and an old bicycle. Tools hung on the walls and there were boxes on the floor, but nothing more. He ran into the darkness, moving from corner to corner, but it was clearly an empty space. He pushed into several small rooms, straining to see in the dark, but encountered nothing but junk.

Behind him, then, he heard a voice, plaintive but getting louder.

'Hello. Excuse me, old chap. Hello.'

He looked around to see the round face of a fat, balding man looking at him through the broken window. They stared at each other in incomprehension for a few long moments. Allen felt the adrenaline dissipate rapidly. He lost his momentum, his anger and his urge to fight. He stared up, realising what he'd done, what it meant, how lost he was, how lost Emily was, somewhere, somewhere else, not here. He was wrong, he was chasing shadows. This was never Roger's address. Roger

was cleverer than that and he was stupid. A strangled sob escaped from his throat.

'What are you doing in my cellar, you silly fucker,' said the
stranger. 'I'm calling the police.'

Emergent

PC Jamie Harrison had joined the force to become a detective but was happy to work his way up the ranks. He enjoyed being a constable, liked the random nature of the work, the day-to-day encounters with members of the public. He didn't even mind the occasional blood and gore, the distressed children or severely damaged adults. To him they were all of a muchness, an essential part of the job.

That day the first call was made back to the West Hampstead police station by Samirah Salib. *'Requesting support for incident at 37 Chilcot Road.'* When asked the nature of the incident she could only repeat, *'People, people, in the cellar.'* She also asked for an ambulance with the comment, *'There's a man here too, but he's gone'.*

Within half an hour it was clear to the news teams of London that a major incident was developing in North London. They dispatched outdoor-broadcast vans with elevating satellite dishes on the roof and news reporters to the scene and jostled for position outside the house where a succession of police, medical and other, unidentified vehicles were converging.

In the early evening twilight the first people were led out with blankets over their heads and, although the police tried to keep a lid on information, reporters on site were quick to establish for themselves some facts. These were soon spreading fast through the wilder reaches of the Internet.

-Scenes of horror in hidden chamber
-Abducted persons held on site
-Multiple persons including children
-One person believed deceased at scene

There was a lot more though.

By midnight an early stage report was on the area commander's desk.

The dead man was named as Roger Standen, the owner of the house, who was now believed to be responsible for the historic abduction and incarceration of his cousin eighteen years previously. There was a strong possibility that he had accomplices and a fast-moving investigation was underway with more arrests expected imminently.

During the night the reports were updated regularly as the picture became clear.

The woman, who had been in the cellar for eighteen years and long presumed dead, was Abigail Standen, a cousin of the dead man.

She had given birth multiple times. Three of her children had survived. They were the product of rapes by her abductor.

The fifth person in the chamber was Emily Morgan, who had gone missing sixty days previously.

The incident was being presumed to be part of an escape attempt by the abductees.

Standen's aunt, who lived in the house and who was present at the time of discovery, had suffered a major medical incident and was in intensive care at an unnamed hospital.

Across the world, word spread fast between taker and keeper. Roger is dead. Roger has gone. In dark cellars and damp basements, in vaults and sealed units, in underground car parks and cells built high above ground, captives passed another dark endless day with no change, but for their captors, things were moving. Nobody knew what Roger had written down, nobody knew what he had left behind.

Sometime around eleven that night Allen flipped open his laptop and glanced at the screen.

Family emerge from underground hell prison

And he knew.

Release

Allen lay full length on the bed in a chilly room which, although sparsely furnished, was decorated with a certain elegance. He hadn't wanted to come out here, to this refuge on the far northern coast run by a released keepen that Jenkins had told him about. She can help you, he said. Eventually, beaten down by grief and loneliness, he'd given in.

The television blared in front of him as he drifted in and out of sleep, desperate not to miss what he was waiting for. His evening proceeded in jumps, programmes seemed to start and then be over without him seeing anything. Finally, what he was really waiting for but also dreading came, and he forced himself back into the waked world, holding his eyelids up manually.

The announcer started up in the hyperventilated manner common to cheap television.

And now, in a coda to one of the most disturbing stories of recent times, we are pleased to bring you The Jenni Ransome Show.

What guests can you offer up to an escaped girl, to someone who learned their trade locked into a cell for their whole childhood, he wondered.

The titles flashed and the camera panned across a studio. There was Jennifer, sitting on a bright upholstered chair in the manner of every chat show host, smiling, bright-eyed and nervous. She had been groomed extensively. She's had surgery, he thought, her face isn't quite moving properly. She held a clip board and Allen felt a flash of pride as she launched into her introduction, telling the world how she'd dreamed of this moment every day of her captivity. And this, he thought, is what The Prick had wanted. This is what he had trained her for, had implanted in her head almost from the first day. The announcer had started up again, almost screaming his autocue as a wiry man bounded out from backstage and Jennifer rose to greet him, to kiss him on both cheeks and gesture him to-wards the large red sofa.

We're delighted to bring you our first guest, ladies and gen-tlemen, please, a big round of applause for the footballer of the year ...

Somewhere, in a grubby flat in a tower block in some third rank English city, a fat man was watching this as well, mouth-ing along and salivating as Jenni spoke her lines, as she turned first to this camera, then that, opening her eyes wide and lean-ing slightly forward to engage with her first minor celebrity.

Allen was already asleep again.

The next morning, he sat alongside a middle-aged woman in a good viewing position, high on the dunes above the flat, waveless water and shielded his eyes against the morning sun. The empty beach seemed to stretch for ever into the distance in both directions before losing its focus in a hazy afternoon light. Children's voices shrieked from the waterline, pale white creatures running up and down and splashing excitedly at the water's edge.

Both the watchers looked worn and tired but, at the same time, dressed as if they were comfortable in their own skins, in their own personalities at their own time. The woman wore a long dress, light purple and white. Her hair was faded red, heaped up on her head and held with pins. Around her eyes deep lines carved into her face, but she retained some poise and beauty. She hugged at her knees as Allen turned back to talk to her.

She smiled at him warmly and he looked into her eyes where he knew he could see her own prison. You can take the keepen out of the cell, he thought, but you can't take the cell out of the keepen.

'How was the show?' she asked.

'Didn't you watch it?'

'I don't have a television, can't watch it,' she said.

'She's alright, she's got what she wants. I guess she's entitled to that, at least. I'm not sure what I got. I've lost Emily. I've lost everything.'

'Well, at least Roger can't hurt anyone else.'

'Fuck Roger, Roger took her to hurt me. Now she'll never come back to me.'

'He was a very dangerous man,' she said.

She put a hand on his arm. 'Don't let them shut you up.'

He shrugged.

'They tore his house apart, shredded everything. They found nothing. No sign, no links to the others. They've all gone into hiding, they all have keepen who won't get out. I couldn't find them. I'm not sure that I ever can now.'

'His kind thought they'd beaten me into silence once,' she said. 'They thought that I would close my eyes and my ears, but here I am.'

The figures from water's edge approached noisily, the small ones running ahead, their mother lagging behind, picking her way slowly up the beach. As they saw him the group became silent.

Then the children ran ahead along the sandy path followed by their mother, leaving Allen and the woman standing on the dunes.

'Come on,' she said. 'Let's get you back to your room.'

About the author

Ivan Pope is a writer, artist and long-distance cyclist who lives in Brighton. He graduated from Goldsmiths College Fine Art BA with the YBA generation and was involved with a number of early internet developments in the UK and across the world. He invented the cybercafe at London's Institute of Contemporary Arts and founded the world's first web magazine, *The World Wide Web Newsletter*. He has taught at art colleges in London, Newport and Brighton. He is now a writer of fiction and psychogeographic non-fiction. He is currently undertaking a PhD in creative non-fiction at Plymouth University.

https://en.wikipedia.org/wiki/Ivan_Pope

Lightning Source UK Ltd.
Milton Keynes UK
UKHW010951100321
380099UK00004B/635